Enjoy the adventure !

WIDE AWAKE
IN
DREAMLAND

JOHN DUEL

WIDE AWAKE IN DREAMLAND

Illustrated by Bruce Burton

Stargaze Publishing
La Verne, California

This book is dedicated to my sister, Trish. Without her gentle—and not so gentle—proddings and her encouragement, I doubt if *Wide Awake in Dreamland* would have made it this far. For that, I am eternally grateful.

ACKNOWLEDGMENTS

The author would like to thank the following people for their efforts in helping him on his journey to complete *Wide Awake in Dreamland* :

David Jamieson, my editor, for playing it straight—and not safe—with me. The book is better than it would have been without your guidance;

Chuck McPherson and Bruce Burton, who breathed life into my characters with the stroke of a brush. Your illustrations are wonderful—and so are you guys;

Ed McGowan, whose friendship and advice got me through the rough spots;

The whole gang at Hang-Ups, especially those whose names I "stole" to create my characters, Benita Favela, Josie Ramirez and Marques Andres;

Jonathan Alburger, Dawn Dolphin, Taryn Wise, Jim Thomas and Reggie Young for providing early manuscript suggestions;

My parents, Walter and Yvonne, for providing the support to make my dream a reality and for believing in me enough to do so;

The librarians, Bea Faust and Jerene Battista, for their comments.

The teachers who spent their classroom time reading my book;

The students, whose faces, comments and letters I shall long treasure;

And, lastly, my sister Trish, to whom this book is dedicated.

Thank you all for making my journey a pleasant one; still, I have only gone one step. . .

TABLE OF CONTENTS

WIDE AWAKE
IN
DREAMLAND

1

EDDIE MEETS
THE SANDMAN

Eddie fought to keep his eyes open. The hum of the car's engine lulled his eyelids shut. Each time they closed, Eddie shook his head to open them again. He didn't want this day to end.

Eddie watched the arcs of red and white auto lights while his father drove, but the lights only made him more tired. He and his father headed south on the 101 freeway toward Palo Alto, where they lived. This evening they watched baseball at the 'Stick—the nickname locals gave Candlestick Park. The last time at the 'Stick, Eddie had endured a boring pitching match-up, but not tonight. Tonight the Giants, in a high-scoring affair, soundly beat their L.A. rivals. But something made tonight's game even more special: all youngsters in attendance received a set of that year's San Francisco Giants baseball cards.

The cards attracted Eddie to the game. He had looked forward to the game knowing he would receive the cards. To get them, he had even lied to his parents about his progress on the science project due Monday, telling them it was coming along and he'd finish it no problem. Well, that wasn't really a lie, he thought, it just wasn't the whole truth. He knew he could finish it over the weekend, and he had given it some thought—and that should count as progress. If he had told his parents that he hadn't done anything for it (when he had known about the project for six weeks), he would have missed the game. "School comes first, young man," they'd say, and that would have been that—no ball game and no cards. Eddie pulled the cards out of his jacket pocket and flipped through the stack again. Yes, it had been worth the risk, he decided.

When Eddie's head dropped forward, he released the cards. He shook his head and picked them up. Maybe he should have told his parents everything he thought as he counted them. No, it was all right, they were all there. He counted again just to make sure. He

put the cards back into the pocket of the jacket
he wore to every Giants game—even the day
games. Eddie learned early that a jacket was
essential to combat the biting bay winds that
haunt the 'Stick. The same winds that had
stolen home runs from Willie Mays, Willie
McCovey and Will Clark stole warmth from
the spectators with equal vengeance.

Eddie's eyelids closed again. Boy, could
he picture himself playing shortstop on that
field. He imagined robbing batters of singles
by leaping for liners or diving for bloopers.
And he saw himself hitting for power—even
against the wind he'd reach the bleachers. His
head dropped forward. . . . And there he stood,
bat in hand, facing Nolan Ryan (who his father
said was the best pitcher ever). Ryan wound up
and delivered; the ball blazed toward the plate.
Eddie swung as if in slow motion. The crisp
crack of the bat striking the ball echoed through-
out the 'Stick. He watched the ball fly skyward,
higher and higher, farther and farther, till—still
rising—it disappeared into the stars. The fans
cheered as he circled the bases. When he entered
the dugout, the cheers turned into chants,
"Eddie! Eddie!" Eddie ran up the dugout stairs
back onto the field. The crowd stood. Eddie
doffed his cap. The chant continued . . . .

"Eddie, wake up son, we're home." His
father's voice and the car's jarring stop chased

away Eddie's dream. His father helped him out of the car and led him into the house.

"I know you've had a busy day, young man, and you'd best get yourself a good night's sleep or I'll never hear the end of it for keeping you up so late."

Eddie's mother preferred day games. She did not like her nine-year-old son out at a ball-park past his bedtime—especially during the school year.

"Thank you for taking me to the ball game, Dad. I had a great time." He hugged his father and they said good-night at Eddie's door, exchanging a bedtime kiss.

Eddie felt grown-up as he entered his room. For the first time in his life, he was up later than his mom. Also, his father hadn't lingered, as his mother would have, to make sure that Eddie changed into his pajamas. Of course, Eddie also missed out on being tucked into bed—something his mother always did. He turned on the light and tossed his Giants cap onto his dresser. He started to take off his jacket, but remembering the cards, he pulled them out instead. "One more look," he said, "and then I'll go to bed."

Eddie went over to his bed, dropped to his knees and reviewed the cards. As he finished with one, he tossed it onto his bed and concentrated on the next. He soon came upon

his favorite player, Joe Ortiz
shortstop. Ortiz played h'
that sports writers comp'
shortstop, Ozzie Smith—the
But to Eddie, Ortiz was the besı.
foot-nine (short by Major League stanuu
Ortiz was a natural underdog. Despite his lack
of height, Ortiz fielded and hit with amazing
skill. His career average, printed in bold on the
back of his card, read .323. "Wow," said Eddie,
reveling in his idol's feat. Eddie could picture
Ortiz snagging a ground ball and firing it to
first base—and Eddie could imagine himself
performing with equal ease. Following Ortiz's
card with his eyes, Eddie placed it on his bed
more carefully than he did the others. That's
when he noticed the strangest thing his young
eyes had yet seen.

There, in the middle of his bed, was a
small mound not more than an inch high. Now
that in itself is not so very strange, although
one might pause to wonder its cause. What
made this bulge unusual was that it actually
moved. Eddie blinked his weary eyes and
looked again. Again he saw the small mound
moving slowly but steadily toward the top of
his bed. Fear mounted as his initial amazement
subsided; for he knew that only a big bug
could cause such a disturbance with his
bedclothes. He jumped to his feet afraid, but

so afraid that he wasn't curious to see just what type of bug it was. Scooping up his baseball cards, he put them back into his pocket. The bug moved to within a foot of his pillow. Now came the time for action. Mustering his courage, Eddie gripped his bed covers and flung them back. What he saw was no bug. At least it didn't look like a bug; although, it must have been one. It had darted under the pillow so quickly that Eddie didn't get a good look; yet, he was sure that he didn't see what was really there. For Eddie thought he saw a man less than one inch tall who, upon seeing him, ran toward the pillow and dove under it headfirst—exactly as a ballplayer would dive back to first base.

Eddie stood still a moment before concluding there was but one thing to do. He lifted the pillow. "Gone." That one word summed up everything; for, indeed, there was nothing on the bed.

Again Eddie pondered. He knew he had seen something hide under his pillow. On impulse, he shifted his eyes from the bed to the pillow in his hands. Again he could not believe his eyes.

Clinging to the pillow, as if for dear life, was the little man whom Eddie thought but refused to believe he had seen. The man had neatly groomed blonde hair and a well-trimmed beard. He wore an outfit of brown,

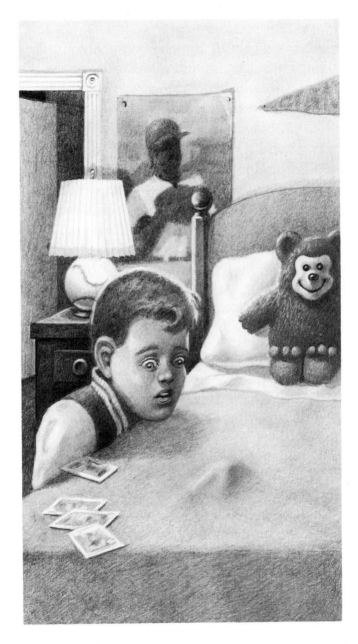

right down to his boots. Fastened to his belt were several small pouches that looked like money bags, each pulled closed at its top by a drawstring. Eddie stood staring at the apparition, quite forgetting that it was real.

"Well aren'tcha gonna put me down?" asked a small, faraway voice.

"What?" Eddie's boomed in comparison.

Indeed, it must have sounded like a shout to the miniature man; for with an even smaller, farther away voice, he said, "Glory be, you needn't talk so, mere whisperin' will do."

"Sorry," whispered Eddie, "but I can hardly hear you. You, sir, must speak up."

"Let me down and up I shall speak," yelled the little figure with a voice that, though still small, sounded closer at least. Eddie obliged his guest, setting him down upon the bed.

"Thankye, thankye," said the little man in as loud a voice as he could muster. In his now audible speech Eddie picked up an accent that most closely resembled an Irish brogue. "Me arms were killin' me they were, hangin' on so high above the bed."

"Who are you?"

"Ah, who indeed. A logical question I grantcha that. One I should have anticipated had I known you'd see me. And I do see that you do see me. You see me!"

Eddie nodded.

"Why, glory be! We expect to be seen, you know. But when it happens we never expect it. So we are forever caught off guard."

"You expect it, but you never expect it?" Eddie had a puzzled look on his face. "What, exactly, do you mean?"

"Aye, an explanation is called for, so let me explain. I meant simply that once in a great while someone from the Real World sees us. That, me friend, takes imagination—not just any imagination, mindcha. A good imagination. Most people don't have that keen an imagination and, sadly, never give us notice. Because we are seen only once in such a great while, when we are seen, we are seen unexpectedly."

"Oh, I see," said Eddie, feeling privileged to be blessed with such a good imagination. "But who are you?"

"Aye, that was yer original question. To answer yer question simply, I am the Sandman."

"Oh," said Eddie. Feeling his question hadn't been answered, he ventured another. "What do you mean by 'the Sandman'?"

"What do I mean by 'the Sandman'?" yelled the Sandman so loudly that Eddie could now hear him without difficulty. "Haven'tcha, after all, heard of me? 'Tis I who comes each night to sprinkle me sand into yer eyes and assure that you're off into the land of dreams. Why, that's me job, lad."

"You mean you're the *actual* Sandman?"

"One and the same," said the Sandman, his pride returning with recognition. "In fact, that's why I was in yer bed just now: I was tryin' to do me job. Imagine me surprise on findin' it empty. What keeps you up into these wee hours, lad?"

Eddie told the Sandman about his evening at the ballpark, with the Sandman asking a question here and there. The conversation alternated between Eddie's soft whisperings, which to the Sandman seemed loud, and the Sandman's loud shoutings, which to Eddie seemed soft.

After Eddie had satisfied the Sandman's curiosity, his own returned. "Hey, if I have such a good imagination, how come I've never seen you before?"

"Why, laddy, that is an easy answer to give: most of the time you're sound asleep and always it is pitch dark when I arrive. Besides, I pride meself on me stealth."

Eddie had no idea what "stealth" meant but figured it had something to do with invisibility, which to Eddie seemed like something worth taking pride in. "Yes, you are tough to see, I see that now," he whispered politely.

"Well, since you do see me, let me make an offer. How wouldcha like to go to Dreamland with me, lad?"

"That's what you do every night, right?"

"To see you reach the land of dreams, aye. That I do and that you'd have no choice over. 'Tis not to the land of dreams but to *Dreamland* that I want to take you."

He said this with so much excitement that Eddie understood Dreamland to be more special than the land of dreams. As to the distinction, though, Eddie remained clueless.

"What's the difference between Dreamland and the land of dreams?"

"Why, only all the difference in the world, lad. The land of dreams is a mere diversion. Things happen there without rhyme or reason. Surely you can remember some of yer dreams?"

"Sure."

"Well, do they always make sense?"

Eddie shook his head and giggled.

"Well, in Dreamland things do make sense. And things happen sequentially. Moreover, entry to Dreamland is allowed by escort only—a Sandman being the only escort. So only someone who sees a Sandman may visit Dreamland. If that someone so chooses. What say you, lad, will you go?"

Seeing it as an honor, Eddie agreed to go. Then a thought struck him. "Are there monsters and witches and scary things?"

"Well, sure," admitted the little man.

"Then I don't want to go."

"I respect yer feelin's, lad, and would not take you where you dare not go. 'Tis too bad, though, for so few actually do have the chance to see Dreamland in all its wonders. I expect I shall run into another with as keen an imagination as yers; though I can't expect this unexpected thing to happen soon." The Sandman paused. "By the by, did I mention that the witches and monsters in Dreamland can do you no harm? Of course, if you don't want to go I understand that."

"You mean the monsters can't actually hurt me?"

"Scare you, aye; hurt you, no. You, lad, will be sound asleep while with me. If frightened, you will simply wake up and return to the safety of the Real World."

The Sandman's sincerity persuaded Eddie. "I'll go," he said in his regular voice, forgetting to whisper.

The poor little man put a hand over each ear. "Whisper, whisper!" he shouted. Then, more enthusiastically, "That is yer final answer then?"

"Yes," whispered Eddie, "I'll go."

"I guarantee you, lad, you shan't be disappointed! Now let's do what must be done and off we'll go to Dreamland."

2

DREAMLAND

"What must I do to get to Dreamland?" whispered Eddie.

"Why, lad, all you have to do is lie down and keep yer eyes closed," the Sandman hollered. "I'll do the rest."

Eddie lay on his bed and closed his eyes as instructed. But being curious, Eddie peeked; since the Sandman stood next to his face, Eddie had to glance askance to watch him. The Sandman took one of the sacks from his belt and pulled it open. Balancing it on one palm, he stuck his other arm inside. When he pulled it out, fine grains of sand sifted through his fingers back into the bag.

"Sand?"

Eddie's whispered question startled the Sandman, who unclenched his fist, letting all of the sand fall back into the bag.

"You, lad, are supposed to keep yer eyes closed and take this lyin' down," said Eddie's escort. "Is that such a hard thing to do?"

"Well, yes, really, it is," Eddie replied. "'Cause I don't know what you're going to do."

"Ah, I see. If I tell you, will you promise to keep yer eyes closed?"

Eddie nodded.

"Very well. I'm gonna take a handful of me special sleepin' sand. Then I will sprinkle it onto yer eyelids. You will immediately fall fast asleep as if in a dream. Butcha won't be dreamin', for you shall be with me in Dreamland. Now close yer eyes."

"Wait," said Eddie. "How can I be asleep *and* with you in Dreamland?"

"Oh bother, I forgot about the Real World's lack of understandin' when it comes to paradoxes," said the Sandman more to himself than to Eddie.

But Eddie heard and did have a lack of understanding, "What is a 'dox'?"

"What is a what?"

"A 'dox'," whispered Eddie. "You said I wouldn't understand a pair of them and I don't even understand one."

Before Eddie had finished, the Sandman rocked back and forth on his back, with his hands on his stomach and his feet in the air, belly up with laughter.

"Ha, ha, ha, 'paradoxes' said I, not a pair of 'doxes.' Ha, ha, ha." It sounded exactly the same to Eddie, so he waited politely for the Sandman to regain his composure.

"A 'paradox,' me lad, is a statement that appears to contradict itself and, therefore, be untrue; yet, seemin' to be untrue, it is true. In other words, you will be fast asleep in yer bed and with me in Dreamland. You will be in two places at the same time!"

"That's impossible," said Eddie. Then after a pause, added, "Isn't it?"

"Seemin'ly impossible, but very possible."

"Well, I still don't get it," said Eddie.

"Let me see if I can put it another way. When you dream, do you ever feel as if you're actually there in yer dream?"

"Sure."

"Well now, while dreamin', you would believe, wouldcha not, that if yer mum came into yer room she would findcha in yer bed?"

"Of course she would cause I'd be sleeping."

"And you'd agree, wouldn'tcha, that you wouldn't see her?"

15

"Right, cause I'd be dreaming."

"I think you'd agree that she wouldn't see yer dream?"

"Of course she wouldn't."

"So both of yer experiences at that same moment, though real, would be very different, wouldn't they?"

"Yes, I'd be dreaming and she'd be watching me sleep."

"That's how it will be now," said the Sandman, holding both hands out in front of him. "Though you, in essence, will be in Dreamland, yer body will be sleepin'. You will see Dreamland; yer mother will see you sleepin' in yer bed. So at the same time, you both see somethin' entirely different. Sounds impossible, yet it is true. Do you understand now?"

"I think so. I will be in bed because I will be sleeping, but I will be in Dreamland because I will be with you. And that's a paradox. What a strange thing a paradox is."

"You, laddy, are wise beyond yer years. Now times a-wastin', so are you ready to close yer eyes?"

"Ready," said Eddie. He shut his eyes.

Eddie heard the Sandman fumbling with the bag containing the special sleeping sand. Eddie felt the tiny man climb onto his face; he felt the Sandman walk up his cheek, stopping at his left eye.

"Do you do this every night?" asked Eddie.

"Aye," said the little man, "now hush."

"How come I've never felt you walking on my face before?"

"Oh, once or twice you have felt me and brushed me off. Sometimes you've rolled over, makin' me job that much more difficult. Now be still so I can finish."

Eddie felt the sand hit first one eyelid and then the other. Instantly relaxed, he rolled onto his side.

"Well, lad, what do you think?"

The voice surprised Eddie. Oh, he recognized it all right, but it was too loud. The little Sandman's loudest yells up to now hadn't reached that volume. Eddie quickly opened his eyes. He saw that he was lying on grass, and not his bed. Eddie blinked his eyes, rubbed his eyes, and blinked his eyes again. Still, the view remained unchanged. Eddie was no longer in his bedroom.

"Where I am?"

Then Eddie noticed a pair of boots a few feet from where he lay. Eddie followed the boots upward past two stubby legs dressed in brown cloth to a belt with many little sacks fastened around it. His eyes raced upwards and saw the bearded face of the Sandman, who now appeared to tower over him.

"You're so big!" whispered Eddie.

"Big, am I?" laughed the little man. "Why, you're lyin' down. Get up if you think I'm big."

Eddie scrambled to his feet. He was still a head taller than the Sandman, but the man *had* increased tremendously in size. "How did you get so big?"

"I'm still shorter than you. Though I admit it has been a long, long time since anyone has called me big. By the way, lad, you needn't whisper here. I am talkin' normal and you can hear me, can'tcha?"

"Why, yes," whispered Eddie; then, "I MEAN, YES. BUT HOW DID YOU GET SO BIG?"

"A common question, I assure you. But the answer is not an easy one to give. As for meself, I'd prefer to say that it's all relative and leave it at that. Besides, lad, there's so much I want to show you and we only have the night. Oh, let me do this right. Welcome to Dreamland, lad!"

Eddie looked around him now. His eyes grew wide with wonder. Eddie had never been to Dreamland before, but he had been to Carmel, on the California coast, and Dreamland reminded him of Carmel. He stood on a reddish bluff with lush, green grass and hundreds of cypress trees. Beyond the bluff, stretching to the horizon, he saw an ocean. Whether it was the ocean or the trees, Eddie thought of Carmel.

"Wow," said Eddie, marveling at the sight.

"Beautiful, isn't it?"

"Oh, yes."

"Well, this is Sandsibar."

"I thought this was Dreamland," said Eddie.

"Well, aye, lad, that is true. But we're on an island in Dreamland. Dreamland is much bigger than this little island. This island is me home and its name is Sandsibar."

"It reminds me of Carmel."

"In the Real World?" asked the Sandman.

"In California," said Eddie.

"Oh, it must be on the coast."

Eddie nodded.

"The coast is not me territory."

"You don't go to the coast?"

The Sandman shook his head.

"What kind of Sandman are you?"

"A busy one, I assure you."

"You can't be too busy if you skip the whole coast."

"Another Sandman covers it."

"You mean there's more than one Sandman?"

"But, of course, lad. Didcha think with so many of you that one of us could do the job alone? 'Tis a big task, me friend. Why, the first thing I'll show you is Sleepy Cove. That's where we Sandmen gather our special sleepin' sand. After that I'll take you to Sandadu, our fabulous city. Then I should show you the Sandbar Willow Forest on the other side of the island. Oh, and you must see Sand Castle. Time keeps marchin'. We better hurry, lad."

Taking Eddie by the hand, he led him down a dirt path toward the beach below. The sand on the beach surprised Eddie, for it shimmered like gold. They walked along the beach around the red bluff that they had come down. At the bend of the bluff, they reached a secluded cove. On these sandy shores, Eddie saw not one or two, but hundreds of bearded men dressed exactly like the one with him. The men looked as if they were harvesting a crop: They worked hunched over, grabbing fistfuls of sand and filling little bags.

"Wow!" said Eddie. "There are so many of you."

"Aye."

"And you're all too big. You can't sneak around that big."

"None of us does, lad. As you have seen."

"Yeah," said Eddie. "But you never told me how you got so big."

The Sandman stopped, still twenty feet from the sand harvesters. He wore the look of defeat. "That question, again? And you want me to answer it, do you?"

Eddie nodded.

"Very well, then. What if I toldcha it were you who were small. Wouldcha understand that?"

Eddie shook his head.

"I didn't think so," continued the Sandman. "In truth, I am bigger *and* you are smaller. By a factor of seven to be exact."

"Huh?" Eddie had a puzzled expression.

"I am seven times bigger than I was in the Real World and you, lad, are seven times smaller. So in yer measurements I am still quite small, less than half a foot high."

"Then how tall am I?" asked Eddie.

"Oh, I'd guess between seven and eight inches."

"Seven or eight *inches*?" Eddie said indignantly.

"Afraid so. From the Real World perspective. But in Dreamland, you're exactly the same height. I'm three-foot-two here and you're still a little more than four feet. At least, usin' our measurements, you are. Like I said earlier, it's all relative."

"There you go again, Sandy," said an accented voice from behind them. Both turned to face the speaker, a wizened little man who walked toward them. A snow-white beard surrounded his wrinkled face.

"Oh, hi, Sam," Eddie's escort said. "I didn't notice you."

"Not that I'd expectcha to, rantin' and ravin' about relativity as you were," said Sam scoldingly. "Don'tcha remember the last time you explained relativity to a young lad? Poor little Albert spent a good many years ponderin' it before he could precisely prove what you told him. We wouldn't want that to happen again, now would we, Sandy?"

Sandy appeared quite ashamed of himself, but Eddie came to his rescue. "It's all right. I think I understand it, anyway. It's just another paradox, that's all."

"Well, I see you brought another bright one with you, Sandy," said Sam. Then bowing to Eddie, he said, "Welcome to Dreamland, me young friend." He nudged Sandy. "Aren'tcha gonna introduce us?"

"Certainly," Sandy answered. Turning to Eddie he said, "Let me introduce you to me boss, Sam."

"Nice to meet you, sir," said Eddie.

When it became apparent to Sam that Sandy wasn't going to introduce the boy to him, he said, "Well?"

"Well what?"

"You didn't get the lad's name didcha, Sandy?"

"No, I'm afraid I forgot."

"You're impossible, Sandy. 'Tis just like you to bring the poor lad to Dreamland without so much as knowin' his name. And what be yer name, son?"

"Eddie, sir."

"Pleased to meetcha, Eddie," said Sam. "And, for goodness sakes, call me Sam. 'Sir' makes me feel old; believe me, I'm too old to be made to feel old as well. By the way, yer escort's name is Sandy."

"You'll have to forgive me, Eddie," said Sandy. "I've only been doin' me job for a couple hundred years and you're only the third person to see me, so I'm inclined to forget introductions."

"You've been doing this for how long?" asked Eddie.

"Precisely one hundred and eighty-three years. No time, really, compared to Sam. He's the most experienced Sandman."

"And we shan't discuss how long I've been at it," said Sam. "What do you plan to show the lad?"

"Everything," said Sandy, sweeping his arms out before him.

"Good," said Sam. "Out of everything, lad, what wouldcha like to see first?"

"I want to see Sand Castle."

"Excellent choice," said Sandy.

A whistle blew. "Why, it's quittin' time for the graveyard shift," said Sam. "Well, to get to Sand Castle you have to go through

Sandadu, our city. Since we're all headin' for Sandadu, we might as well join you."

"That would be wonderful," said Eddie.

And so Eddie headed toward the city of Sandadu surrounded by hundreds of Sandmen. Sandy walked on his right and Sam on his left. Eddie was enjoying himself. He towered over all of the Sandmen. And with their strange accents, the Sandmen were fun to listen to. They chatted on and on about sand. The quality of the day's harvest and the quantity. Oh, occasionally someone would mention how odd it was to have a visitor from the Real World, but soon the topic would return to sand. Didn't the texture seem more coarse today than usual? Several times Eddie mentioned Sandadu and each time the Sandmen would say a polite word or two about the city before turning the conversation back to sand. Didn't it seem exceptionally shiny and light today?

Eddie inwardly rejoiced at his decision to come to Dreamland. He laughed at how foolish he had been in his bedroom just moments before, worrying about monsters and witches and scary things. Having arrived in Dreamland, Eddie could see no possible danger in such a perfect place.

3

DANGER AHEAD

At the crest of the hill, the city of Sandadu came into view.

"Wow," exclaimed Eddie. Sandadu's buildings, made from a mixture of Sandsibar's red soil and gold sand, glittered in the sunlight below them. Eddie could see the whole city. It sprawled out to the hills on one side and the ocean on the other. Eddie hurried down the trail, followed by the Sandmen.

When he reached the city, he walked along a boulevard of gold cobblestones. To Eddie, Sandadu looked like a miniature city, consisting of scaled down buildings built to accommodate its tiny inhabitants. It didn't quite look real, but that only made it all the more interesting to him.

"This is Sandadu, the city we pride. Welcome to it," Sandy said with a sweep of his arm.

"Aye, welcome to it," said six or eight other Sandmen before resuming their conversation about sand.

"You should be proud of it," Eddie said. "It's beautiful."

"I'm delighted to find our young friend has such good taste," said Sam. "It does me heart good and restores me faith in the younger generation."

Eddie looked from one building to the next. Each had rounded windows and doors, and a sloping, thatched roof. The buildings were far from tall and far from wide, but not far from each other. They made Sandadu a quaint city. Despite its quaintness (and some would say because of it), Sandadu emanated beauty.

The group made their way down the boulevard. At each corner a few Sandmen would break away from the crowd, explaining that they lived down that street. Each would say, "Nice meetin' you," to Eddie before hurrying off, discussing sand. A large number of Sandmen still surrounded Eddie when the group reached Town Square. A reddish sidewalk surrounded Town Square. Within the square there was but one building. Grass filled the remaining area.

"That building is our City Hall," said Sandy, pointing.

"Neat," said Eddie, who liked Town Square.

Suddenly, in front of them, a cloud of black smoke rose. As it did, Sandmen began screaming and scattering, running in all directions. Of all the Sandmen, only Sandy and Sam stayed by Eddie, but they also had wanted to run. When the smoke cleared, Eddie knew why. In front of him, he saw the most frightening man he'd ever seen.

"Sound the alarm, sound the alarm!" yelled many a Sandman. Immediately a loud bell, which sounded like a fire alarm, pealed forth from City Hall.

Fear froze Eddie in an unenviable position three feet in front of the apparition. Although all this commotion happened within an instant, Eddie had gotten a good look at the man. He did not like what he had seen. The man, dressed in black, had ashen gray skin which, in places, was tinged a slightly greener gray. He had a vulturelike posture, slanting forward from the middle of his back. His long nose extended three to four inches from his face. His beady black eyes were so bloodshot they shone red when hit by the sun. When this vile creature opened his mouth to speak, he revealed teeth ranging from shades of yellow-brown to greenish-black.

"I shall be brief and to the point," he said in a deep, chilling tone. "Give me the boy." The speaker extended his right hand as if expecting his request to be granted instantly. All Eddie saw were his fingernails: yellow and dirty.

Eddie, Sam and Sandy stood shaking. Despite his knocking knees, Sandy defiantly said, "We will not!"

Those three words seemed to infuriate the ugly man. He narrowed his eyes and clenched his fists. Giving Sandy a concentrated glare, he unclenched his fists, holding his hands out palm up. Then he raised them to his chin. As he did so, Sandy let out a "Whoa!" and spread out his arms for balance as he rose helplessly above the ground. With a sudden motion the man in black thrust both hands outward. Sandy flew backwards head over heels through the air, screaming. He hit the ground some twenty feet away, somersaulting to a stop.

Then the man in black turned his glare to Sam. In the same voice he commanded, *"Give me the boy!"*

"For goodness sakes, Mortimer, it has been a long time," said Sam, trying to sound conversational.

"I don't have time to chat," Mortimer said. Indeed, the alarm still rang out, and in the distance a siren could now be heard. "GIVE ME THE BOY!"

"Of course we will," Sam said.

Sandy, rubbing his head and looking dazed, had just rejoined his two friends. Sam's reply startled him. "Oh, no we won't!" Sandy directed his response to Sam, not Mortimer.

"Hush, Sandy," Sam said, brushing the younger man back with his arm. "Mortimer and I go back to days before you were ever born. He is not a man to be taken lightly, so let me handle him."

"The old fool speaks wisely for once," said the evil man with a sneer. "Now don't try my patience any longer."

"We shan't," said Sam. His reply made Eddie anxious.

"What about me?" Eddie asked wide-eyed. "I don't want to go with this guy."

Although Eddie had spoken to his friends, Mortimer answered. "You already made up your mind. When you chose to come to Dreamland, you chose to join me."

"I did not!" said Eddie, frightened.

"Hush, lad," whispered Sam. The sirens, growing louder by the second, seemed to give Sam courage. Addressing Mortimer, Sam said, "Before we turn him over to you, I have but one question. You and I both know thatcha haven't been to Sandadu for many years; yet now, for this young boy, you return. Me question is: Why?"

"Why? I'll tell you why," said Mortimer, "but knowing can do you no good at all. He has what I crave, and what I shall have—an imagination."

"An imagination!" said Sam. "But his imagination can do you no good, no good whatsoever."

Mortimer apparently found this remark humorous, for he threw back his vulturelike head and laughed. His laugh shocked Eddie by its volume and with its evil tone. But his laugh stopped the instant the sirens ceased behind him. He spun to look.

Eddie also looked. Eddie had been too scared to let his glance wander far from the man in black, but now he watched as a horse-drawn carriage pulled to a halt. This red carriage looked like an old-fashioned fire cart. Two Shetland ponies pulled it; six Sandmen rode it. When it stopped, five of them jumped off. Three ran toward the villain; two ran the other way. All five uncoiled a fire hose as they ran. The two running the other way stopped in front of a fire hydrant. One of these two held the hose in place while the other turned a wrench to tighten it to the hydrant.

"We've wasted too much time," said Mortimer. "Give me the boy and be quick about it."

"He can do you no good," said Sam.

"Fool! You forget that I, Mortimer, am the most powerful being in all of Dreamland. I tampered with your special sleeping sand. I cast a delightfully evil spell upon it that would bring a keen imagination to me—"

The sound of rushing water brought his speech to a sudden halt. Again he spun around. The three firefighters who ran, hose in hand, toward Mortimer had planted themselves ten feet from him, aiming their hose right at him. The hose grew bigger as the water rushed from the hydrant toward the nozzle. Mortimer, his back toward Eddie, his face toward the firefighters, clenched his fist and growled. A black cloud rose and as it dissipated, Eddie could see that Mortimer had vanished. Then the water hit the smoke. And not only the smoke, but Eddie and his two friends as well. The force of the water knocked Eddie, Sam and Sandy backwards. The three firefighters holding the hose also lost their footing and fell to the ground, struggling with the hose.

"That was close," said Sam as he got to his feet.

Yet even before he finished, another black cloud rose on the top of City Hall. Again Mortimer appeared. The three firefighters attempted—with much effort and very little result—to re-aim the powerful hose at him.

While they fought to control it, Mortimer's evil voice boomed above everything else, "I shall have him yet; mark my words. It is useless to try to stop me. Remember, I brought his imagination into Dreamland and it shall be mine."

Sandy pointed out the flaw in his argument: "His keen imagination accounts for his visit. Not yer spell. In Dreamland, Eddie is safe from harm."

"True, his keen imagination *is* why he's here. And, if he were sleeping, I could do him no harm. If he were sleeping, he would be safe. *If he were sleeping.* But therein lies the delight of my spell: the boy is wide awake!" Mortimer threw back his head and laughed his deep, evil laugh. "No one can help him!" Then another black cloud appeared and evil, as fast as it had come, was gone.

The Sandmen who had run off at Mortimer's arrival began returning. Town Square had become a muddy mess. The firefighters, wet and dirty, shut off their water and packed up their equipment.

"Who was that evil man?" asked Eddie, water dripping from his jacket. "And why were you trying to soak him?"

"One question at a time, lad," said Sandy, dripping wet.

"Aye," said Sam, drenched but nodding, "'tis a bit easier that way."

"Sorry," said Eddie. "Who was he?"

"That was Mortimer," Sandy said, "the most wicked, despicable character in all of Dreamland. He is, of course, a warlock."

"A what?" asked Eddie.

"A warlock," repeated Sandy.

"Aye," said Sam, "that's a male witch."

"Which is why we were tryin' to soak him with water," said Sandy. "As everyone knows, witches melt when hit with water."

Eddie nodded, for he knew that was true. "Well, what does he want with my imagination? Why can't he be happy with his own?"

"One question at a time, lad."

"Aye," said Sam.

"Sorry," said Eddie. "Why isn't he happy with his own imagination?"

"Mortimer doesn't have an imagination."

"Aye," said Sam. "No witch does, you know."

Eddie shook his head, for he didn't know that.

"Which is why he wants yers," said Sandy. "With an imagination, Mortimer could do anything."

"Aye," said Sam, "and no one could stop him."

"What worries me, lad," said Sandy, "is that Mortimer has not shown his face on Sandsibar for many years now—ever since his sister melted. In the meantime, we've set up an alarm system to bring out firefighters at a moment's notice."

"Aye," said Sam. "That's why I pretended to go along with Mortimer. To buy some time."

"But he can't harm you, Eddie," Sandy said. "At least not so long as you are asleep."

"Aye," said Sam. "But heaven forbid if you be wide awake."

"Wide awake! That's impossible," said Sandy. Then, taking a lesson from Eddie, he added, "Isn't it?"

"Aye," said Sam, nodding, " 'Tis impossible."

"From what I've seen of Dreamland," said Eddie, "it seems like anything is possible."

"Aye," said Sam with a nod, "that seems quite possibly possible."

"And so what if I am awake? What's the worst thing that can happen to me?"

"The worst thing," Sandy said, "is that Mortimer steals yer imagination, thereby killin' you."

Eddie had asked for the worst, yet this answer was even worse than he had expected. He thought for a few moments. "Then I won't let him take it. But how do I get back home."

"Wide awake, you can't," said Sandy.

"Me lad," said Sam, "I think you misunderstand the true danger. It's not just Mortimer stealin' yer imagination that's a problem if you be wide awake. Once someone in the Real World tries to wake you and cannot, you will perish. And believe me, they won't be able to wake you, if you're not asleep."

"You mean, in the morning I'll die?" cried Eddie with the sudden realization that things were even worse than he imagined.

"Yes, in the mornin' *yer* time," said Sandy. "That's the bad news. Luckily, in Dreamland we have seven hours to each of the Real World's one."

"Aye, lad," said Sam, "so there is time. But if Mortimer is lying—and I hope he is— then you have nothin' at all to worry yer head over."

"So am I awake or not?" asked Eddie.

"Aye," said Sam, "that be the question for the day. And on Sandsibar there's only one man wise enough to answer that question."

"King Solomon!" said a hundred Sandmen in unison.

"Aye," said Sam, nodding in agreement. "King Solomon."

"Who is King Solomon?" asked Eddie.

"Only the wisest man, by far, on Sandsibar," said Sandy. "He lives at Sand Castle, lad, and that be quite a journey from here."

One firefighter began unhitching the two Shetland ponies that had pulled the cart. "You can have our ponies, lad. They'll getcha there quicker."

Eddie and Sandy both thanked him.

"Sandy," said Sam, "you take good care of the lad, you hear? And Eddie, me friend, whatsoever you do, stick with Sandy. Sandy broughtcha to Dreamland and you need him with you to get back to the Real World. And take care of yerself."

Sandy and Eddie got on the ponies and rode away from Town Square heading toward Sand Castle.

4

SAND
CASTLE

Eddie rode on his pony next to Sandy, letting the little man lead. Eddie worried about what would happen to him if Mortimer had brought him to Dreamland wide awake. Maybe he was worrying for nothing, he thought. Maybe he wasn't wide awake at all. But something about Mortimer made Eddie feel uneasy.

They had been riding for well over an hour when Sandy said, "There she be."

Eddie looked up, seeing Sand Castle in the distance. "Wow," he said. It stood above the ocean, at the end of a long, narrow peninsula that had sheer cliffs cutting down either side. These cliffs grew higher as the land extended outward to the sea. Waves beat at the foot of the cliffs.

They quickened the pace of their ponies.

Reaching the peninsula, they rode up it toward a large wall and a moat, which surrounded the castle. Riding beside the moat, Eddie noticed that it was filled with what looked like boiling crude oil. Expecting a foul odor to come from it, he was surprised to smell licorice. The wall also surprised him; since it was only about fifteen feet away, he could clearly see that it was made of sand. So, too, from all appearances, was the castle. But that didn't make any sense to Eddie. It would be foolish to actually build a castle of sand.

"Sand Castle isn't made out of sand, is it?" he asked.

"But, of course, it is, lad. Why do you think we call it *Sand* Castle?"

"But water can wash it away." Eddie's experiences with sand castles came from spending summer days on the beach at Santa Cruz. He knew what the tides did to his castles.

"Aye, but our castle's weakness is its greatest strength. Though water can easily destroy it, Mortimer would never dream of usin' water; for he would also destroy himself. The castle's weakness is his weakness and is, therefore, a strength."

"But doesn't it ever rain?"

"No, lad. Not here. Mortimer stopped the rain long ago. Only the Perpetual Rain

Forest still receives rain. Oh, and Big Mountain gets snow."

Eddie accepted the answer. And he could see that Sand Castle, being so high above the ocean, didn't need to worry about waves.

Sandy pulled up in front of a gate, Eddie stopping beside him. Standing up in his saddle, Sandy cupped his hands and yelled, "Yo, Keeper of the Gate, open up."

From behind the wall a voice shouted back, "Who wishes to enter the home of the king?"

"'Tis I, Sandy, and me Real World friend, Eddie."

"A Real World visitor," said the voice from inside the wall. A peephole in the gate across from Eddie and Sandy opened and an eye peered out. The owner of the eye was apparently satisfied with what he had seen, for a drawbridge was lowered, allowing Eddie and Sandy to ride across it.

As they did, Eddie was amazed at the width of the walls—they must have been at least ten feet thick. He turned his attention to the castle. "Wow!" he said. Sand Castle was about fifty feet high and had seven cylindrical towers that reached even closer to the sky. One turret stemmed from each corner of the castle, while three more towers of varying height were clustered in the middle.

Eddie did not expect to see so many Sandmen in the courtyard. Four of them began to crank up the drawbridge, while two others rushed to help Eddie and Sandy dismount. Two more led the Shetland ponies away. There must have been dozens of them, all dressed in kelly green uniforms. Yet despite their large numbers, there was little activity: Most of the Sandmen just stood straight, with their arms at their sides.

The Sandman who had shouted over the wall to them introduced himself. "I'm the Second Shift Gate Keeper. The king will be glad to have a visitor from the Real World, very glad, indeed."

"Well, I hope so," said Sandy. "The lad may be wide awake. So we'd like to see the king right away."

"Certainly," said the Second Shift Gate Keeper. "You picked a good time to arrive, I must say, a good time, indeed. The king is just about to have lunch and surely you must join him, aye, join him you must. Wide awake, you say? Hmm, I've never heard of such a thing." Then he called, "Main Path Escort of the Forty-Second Escort Squad, some visitors await."

Another little man immediately joined them. He led Eddie and Sandy down the path toward the castle. At both sides of this path, Sandmen stood at attention.

"What are they doing?" Eddie asked Sandy in a whisper.

"Why, lad, they're there for pomp and circumstance. It befits a king."

"Oh," said Eddie.

At the castle the Main Path Escort of the Forty-Second Escort Squad knocked upon the double doors.

"Who goes there?" said a voice from within.

" 'Tis I, the Main Path Escort of the Forty-Second Escort Squad. I'm escortin' two visitors who wish to see the king. Open up, Southern Door Watcher of the Midday Division."

The door swung open. "Me goodness, unless I miss me mark, we have a Real World visitor."

"Aye," said Sandy, "the lad's from the Real World."

"I'm from California," said Eddie.

"How excitin'! The king will be so pleased," said the Southern Door Watcher of the Midday Division. "Come in, come in!"

Eddie had to duck to enter the castle. Built for the Sandmen, the hall had a very low ceiling. Luckily, it was slightly curved, giving Eddie a little more room in the center. He rubbed his hand across the coarse wall, knocking some sand to the ground. It really is made of sand, he thought.

"Let me getcha some Hall Walkers," said the Southern Door Watcher of the Midday Division. He turned and yelled, "Hall Walkers One and Two of the Royal Lunchtime Brigade, visitors await."

Two Sandmen standing only five feet away walked forward. They stopped in front of Sandy and Eddie, gave a little bow and said, "Follow us, please." Eddie had to walk hunched over as he followed the Hall Walkers down the corridor. Every five feet he and Sandy passed a pair of Sandmen, one on either side of the hall.

"Are they just standing around for pompous circumstance, too?" Eddie asked.

"No lad, for security. They are Hall *Watchers* and their job is to watch the halls to make sure each guest is accompanied by a Hall Walker who walks the hall."

"There's certainly enough of them," said Eddie.

"It suits the security and protection of a king," said Sandy.

Reaching a big gold door at the end of the hall, one of the Hall Walkers knocked.

"Who seeks to enter the chamber of his royal highness, the king?" inquired a voice from within.

" 'Tis I, the Number One Hall Walker of the Royal Lunchtime Brigade—I have a visitor."

"And I, the Number Two Hall Walker of the Royal Lunchtime Brigade—I also have a visitor."

The voice from within questioned, "Number One, what color be the clouds today?"

"The clouds, as usual, be gray. But the sky is blue."

"That will do from you. Number Two, the sky above, what is its hue?"

"Above the skies are mostly blue. But the clouds are gray."

"Yer answer, also, is okay," said the man from within. The door swung open. "Can't be too careful these days." The voice belonged to an elegantly dressed Sandman wearing a gold costume with puffs at the shoulders. Eddie eyed him with interest, but when he looked beyond the little man, he was even more amazed. "Wow!" he said. The interior of this room shone completely with gold. The room had a high ceiling—a rarity in Sandsibar. It served as a royal hallway, longer than it was wide. At either side were four gold doors, with one more door at the opposite end. Two royal chamberlains, all dressed alike, stood next to each door. (Chamberlains had the most important duty in all of Sand Castle: They were responsible for the king's well-being. There were, therefore, more of them than all other servants combined—in fact, the Official

Bookkeeper of the King had at last count lost count as to exactly how many chamberlains the king had.)

"A visitor from the Real World! What can I do for you?" the chamberlain asked.

"We'd like to see the king, please," said Eddie.

"The lad may be wide awake," added Sandy.

"Ah," said the chamberlain. "Well, King Solomon will be pleased to see you, I'm sure." The chamberlain led them to the third door on the right. "As you probably heard, the royal luncheon is bein' prepared. You shall be the king's guests. Since it is only lunch, you will be seated in the small dinin' room. I hope you don't mind."

He opened the door to an immense dining room with white walls and gold chandeliers. While another chamberlain led them into this "small" dining room, Eddie wondered what the large one must look like. In the middle of the room was an elegantly carved table. Eddie had never seen such a enormous table before, it must have been over sixty feet long with one hundred chairs around it. The chamberlain seated Eddie and Sandy near the head of the table. Eddie was seated just one chair away from the king's chair, which was much larger than others.

"The king will join us shortly," said the chamberlain as he pushed Eddie's seat in for him.

A hush fell over the room as eight trumpeters entered. They blasted out a little theme after which one of them exclaimed, "Welcome his royal highness, King Solomon the Four Hundred and Eighty-First!"

All lunch guests rose, so Eddie did the same. He whispered to Sandy, "Isn't four hundred and eighty-one a lot of King Solomons?"

"I suppose it is at that, but every king of Sandsibar is named Solomon, since there is no wiser name to give a king."

Just then, Eddie witnessed the arrival of that most trusted and wise monarch himself. King Solomon entered the room wearing a purple satin outfit with gold trim. The outfit bulged tremendously around his midsection leading Eddie to believe that the king really enjoyed his lunches—and probably his breakfasts and dinners, too. Behind him draped a long cape that ten chamberlains held so it wouldn't touch the ground. He came in only steps away from the head of the table through a door at that side of the room. He paused at his chair, gave as much of a bow as his stomach would allow, and then waited while his chamberlains maneuvered his cape over his chair. As he sat down, so did his hundred guests.

One chamberlain who had entered with the king sat in the seat between Eddie and the king. He was the first to speak to Eddie.

"Good afternoon," he said. Then he turned to the king, and said, "Yer royal highness has a visitor from the Real World joinin' you for lunch."

"Splendid!," King Solomon boomed. "Why this is excitin', very excitin' indeed. It has been a long, long time since a visitor from the Real World has had enough of an imagination to visit us. Why, I remember clearly the last visitor, a young lad about eight or nine, by the name of . . . by the name of . . . Sir Stanley, by just what name was that lad called?"

Sir Stanley, the chamberlain who began this conversation, said, "Steven, I believe, yer majesty."

"Was it? Oh, quite right, Steven, it was," said the king with excitement. "Nice lad, too. Kept talkin' about creatures from outer space. Wonderful imagination, that one." Then turning to Sir Stanley, he asked to be introduced to this unexpected guest.

Sir Stanley flushed a little at the realization that he didn't know Eddie's name, but quickly recovered, saying, "I will do one better than that, yer highness. Allow me to

allow yer young visitor to introduce himself."
Nudging Eddie, he said, "Introduce yerself to
the king, lad."

Eddie, overcoming the mixed emotions of
awe and shyness, said, "My name is Eddie,
your highness."

"Splendid, Eddie," the king said, "and
what is it that brings you to Sand Castle?"
Before Eddie could answer, however, the king
went on, "Never mind that now." He gestured
as if waving off a fly. "Reasons can wait till
after lunch, stomachs cannot. Besides, a full
stomach makes for a more sensible head."

"Well said, yer greatness, well said," Sir
Stanley said. The king then snapped his
fingers and the trumpeters blared again.
Several chamberlains immediately brought in
the royal lunch. And what a lunch it was! It
was such a lunch that calling it "lunch" did it
disservice: "feast" would be more appropriate.
The feast consisted of turkey, ham, roast lamb,
pork roast, roast beef, buttered corn, broccoli
with cheese sauce (and various other
vegetables which Eddie politely refused),
yams, baked potatoes, mashed potatoes,
French fried potatoes, potato salad, coleslaw,
green salad, spinach salad (which Eddie also
turned down), and various fruits and breads
too numerous to list. To drink they had Eddie's
favorite, root beer. The sight and smell of all

the food made Eddie realize how hungry he was. Forgetting his worries, he ate heartily and happily.

After the guests finished the main course, chamberlains brought out plates containing desserts: apple pie, boysenberry pie, pumpkin pie, cherry pie, cherries jubilee (which, because it was served flaming, Eddie refused for fear of being burned), chocolate mousse, cheesecake, chocolate cake, pineapple upside down cake, brownies, cookies and fifty-five different flavors of ice cream. Eddie tried as many desserts as he could, before he felt he could eat no more. He was stuffed.

After dessert, chamberlains cleared the table. King Solomon, his stomach satisfied, decided to do the same for his curiosity. "Tell us, now, uh . . . uh . . . tell us yer name again, lad, in case some of the guests have forgotten."

"Eddie."

"Is it? Oh, right. Now tell us, Eddie, what brings you to Sand Castle?"

"I came, sir, because I need your help. I was told that you're the wisest person in all of Dreamland and that if you couldn't help me no one could."

"Wise words, those, and true," the king said in his booming voice. "And why do you require my help?"

"Well, you see, yer majesty," said Sandy, "the lad may be wide awake."

"Impossible, ridiculous." Then the king laughed and as he laughed so did ninety-eight of his one hundred guests—Eddie and Sandy being the only exceptions. The king raised his hand, all laughter ceased. Forcing a serious expression, he said, "Wide Awake? Really now." The king could hold it in no longer. Again he burst out laughing. So did ninety-eight of his guests.

5

___

WIDE
AWAKE!

___

"Pray tell, Sandy," said King Solomon, once more controlling his laughter, "what makes you think the lad is wide awake?" The king held back a giggle with his hand. Many a chuckle, snicker and guffaw came from around the table.

"Well, yer highness, I say it mostly because Mortimer said it."

All giggles, chuckles, snickers and guffaws stopped, replaced by gasps of horror.

"Mortimer?" asked the king. "What do you mean Mortimer said it."

"He appeared in Town Square—"

"Mortimer appeared?" interrupted King Solomon, amid more gasps. "Surely you must be mistaken."

"I only wish I were, yer highness."

"He came with a puff of smoke," said Eddie, flinging his hands up to illustrate the smoke.

"Sounds like Mortimer, all right," said the king. "This is terrible, just terrible."

"Yer highness," whispered Sir Stanley, "it might be nice to know exactly what Mortimer had to say."

"Would it?" whispered the king. Then, in his booming voice he said, "Of course, it would. Tell us, Sandy, *exactly* what Mortimer had to say."

"Exactly? Well, I doubt I could say exactly." Sandy had a thoughtful look on his face.

"Approximately, then" said Sir Stanley to King Solomon.

"Will that do?" asked the king. "Oh, I suppose it will. Approximately, then, Sandy."

"He said he cast a spell on our sleepin' sand which brought Eddie to Dreamland wide awake."

"That's all he said?" asked the king.

"Approximately," said Sandy.

"He also said he wanted my imagination, sir."

"Oh, he said that, too," said Sandy.

"The lad's imagination?" said the king. "What on Sandsibar would he want that for?"

Sir Stanley whispered into the king's ear.

"Well, of course, I know witches don't have imaginations. Everyone knows that. But what does he want one for?"

Again Sir Stanley whispered. "He could do anything imaginable?" asked the king. Sir Stanley nodded. "Why this *is* serious!" said the king. Sir Stanley nodded.

"Will you help me?" asked Eddie. "Please, sir."

"It seems I should," the king said loudly. Then in a whisper to Sir Stanley, he said, "What should I do?"

"It seems to me, yer highness," said Sir Stanley, "thatcha would think of somethin'. Some way of discoverin', for example, whether the lad is truly wide awake."

"Aye," said King Solomon. "That sounds good. Tell me, lad, were you in the least bit frightened when Mortimer came?"

"I was more frightened than I've ever been in my whole life."

"There you have it," said the king. "I'm afraid you're wide awake."

"Excuse me, yer highness," said Sir Stanley in a whisper, "but yer reasonin' is, perhaps, faulty."

"Is it? Well, perhaps, it is," said the king, "but it seems reasonable to me. If he were frightened, he should have woken up, returnin' safely to the Real World. He didn't, so he must be awake."

"However," said Sir Stanley, "I'm sure I needn't remind yer highness of the many documented cases concernin' people who were sound asleep and stayed that way through some pretty scary events."

"Many cases?" asked the king. "How interestin'. Lad, you may not be wide awake, after all."

"So, you're sayin' the lad may or may not be wide awake," said Sandy.

"Precisely," said the king. "And thank you so much for joinin' me for lunch." The king started to rise.

"But which is it, sir?" asked Eddie.

King Solomon sat back down. "You want me to tell you for certain that it's one or the other?"

"It would be most helpful, yer highness," said Sandy.

"Mortimer's visit was risky and imprudent," said Sir Stanley. "He must believe he can take the lad's imagination to justify such a risk. After all, Mortimer may be evil and powerful, but he is no fool."

"That's true," said King Solomon. "Why, if anything, I am more of a fool than Mortimer is, and I'm the *wisest* man on Sandsibar."

Many a "true, true" came from around the table.

"But yer highness," said Sir Stanley, "there lives one more *learned* than yerself."

"You mean old Sherman?" asked the king. Sir Stanley nodded. "Of course, you do. But how can he help us?"

"Me lord," whispered Sir Stanley, "if anyone on Sandsibar knows about the *Book of Spells*, it would be Sherman. He has spent many a year studyin' it."

"Oh," the king said in his booming voice, "how silly of me. We must see old Sherman. He is the oldest livin' Sandman and a great scholar. He would know if it were possible to cast such a spell. Sandy and Sir Stanley will accompany me and . . . and . . . uh . . . me and the lad."

That said, the king rose unsteadily from his chair. Ten chamberlains rushed to arrange the cape draping from his back. Eddie followed Sandy who followed Sir Stanley who followed the ten chamberlains who followed King Solomon who, luckily, knew where he was going. He led them up the winding staircase of one of Sand Castle's towers. King Solomon stopped every few steps to catch his royal breath. (Climbing stairs was more exercise than he was used to.) At the top of the stairs they reached a door.

King Solomon knocked. There was no answer. The king knocked louder. Still no answer. Then he regally pounded the door. To no avail. Sir Stanley pushed past the ten chamberlains and opened the door. King Solomon squeezed into the room. The ten chamberlain quickly followed. Then Sir Stanley and Sandy entered. Eddie went in last. The ceiling was so low he had to crouch. Standing in the room was uncomfortable, but at least it made Eddie feel big.

At the far end of the room, behind a mahogany desk, sat the old Sandman, Sherman. Eddie had never seen someone who looked as old as Sherman looked. ("Old" is, perhaps, too polite a term for Sherman: he was ancient.) Sherman had gray hair and layers upon layers of wrinkles. He wore glasses which magnified his blue eyes to the size of half-dollars.

"Why didn'tcha knock?" Sherman said.

"We did, Sherman, me friend, butcha didn't hear us," said the king.

"Eh?" said Sherman. Sir Stanley brought over a megaphone for King Solomon to use. Sherman refused to admit that his hearing was going, so he never used hearing aides; luckily, his sight was not what it once was, so he never noticed if his visitors cheated.

"I said, we did knock." The king spoke through the megaphone, which amplified

56

his voice so much that Eddie wanted to hold his ears.

"Never mind about knockin'," the ancient Sandman said. "I accept yer apology for bargin' in, yer highness. You are always welcome, you know. Now what can I do for you?"

"We need to know if it be possible for Mortimer to cast a spell on our special sleepin' sand which would bring someone to Dreamland wide awake?"

"Hypothetically speakin', most certainly. Theoretically, quite possibly. Actually, I doubt it. Why do you ask?"

"Because we have a lad from the Real World whose imagination Mortimer wants."

"The lad and his imagination are safe in Dreamland," said Sherman, "as long as the lad is asleep. But if Mortimer found a spell to bring him here awake, then he's in danger. Didcha mention a spell?"

"Aye," said King Solomon.

"What nature of a spell?" asked Sherman.

"What nature of a spell?" King Solomon asked Sir Stanley.

"That's what we want Sherman to tell us, yer highness."

"We do? Oh, of course, we do." Then through the megaphone the king said, "That's what we were hopin' you could tell us, Sherman."

"Well, if a spell were cast, it will be in the *Book of Spells*," said Sherman, pointing to a book on a counter across the room. "Couldcha bring me that book."

Sir Stanley, with Sandy's help, carried the book to Sherman's desk. The book was the thickest Eddie had ever seen, easily four times the size of a complete, unabridged dictionary. Indeed, this book must have been ten thousand pages long. The gold letters stamped into the book's leather cover read "Book of Spells."

Sherman pulled out a magnifying glass and began turning the pages. "Let's look under 'Sand.'" After glancing through five or six pages, he looked up. His eye, doubly magnified by the magnifying glass, was the size of a pancake. "Nothin' there. Let's try 'Special Sleepin' Sand.'" Again, he scanned several pages and again he said, "Nothin'. I'm afraid it could be under almost anything. 'Cursin' Sleepin' Sand,' 'Castin' a Spell on Sand,' or any number of entries. Unfortunately, I am not as learned a student of this book as Mortimer. I've chosen many studies, he has chosen but one. Without knowin' exactly which spell was used, I can be of no help. Without knowin' exactly what Mortimer did to the sand, I'm afraid I cannot discover the proper spell."

"He tampered with it," said Eddie. "He said so himself."

"In those *exact* words?" asked the king.
Eddie nodded.

"He tampered with it, Sherman," the king said through the megaphone.

"Tamperin', hmm," said Sherman. "Well it's certainly worth a try." He flipped the book open and read spells that began with 'tampering.' "Ah," he said at last, "here it is. 'Tamperin' with Sleepy Cove's Special Sleepin' Sand.'" He read in silence for a while. Then he frowned.

"Well?" asked King Solomon.

"This is very serious, very serious, indeed. If he is wide awake, as Mortimer claims, the lad is in imminent danger and time is short."

"Aye, we know that. But how do we know if he is awake or asleep?" asked Sandy. King Solomon relayed the question.

"How indeed," said the pensive scholar. He sat quietly for several moments before he spoke. "I think I may have an idea. With yer majesty's permission." Sherman beckoned for the king to come forward. King Solomon leaned right up into Sherman's face. Sherman whispered his idea into the king's ear, whereupon the king burst out laughing.

"Splendid," said King Solomon. "That will, indeed, do it! Sir Stanley, I have somethin' for you to do."

"What is it I can do for you, sire?" asked Sir Stanley.

"Well, actually, I don't wantcha to do anything *for* anyone; I'd like you to do somethin' *to* someone." Again the king began to laugh. "By jove, I think it will work. I wantcha to pinch our little visitor."

"Excuse me, yer highness?" asked Sir Stanley.

"You heard me, Sir Stanley. I wantcha to pinch our visitor."

"If you say so," Sir Stanley said. He moved in position behind Eddie, who still stood crouched over in the room.

"Wait!" shouted Sherman as Stanley prepared to pinch Eddie. "When the lad is pinched he must answer honestly as to whether he can feel it or not."

"Understand?" asked the king. A reluctant Eddie nodded. Sir Stanley also nodded, saying, "Aye, that will work."

"And," shouted Sherman, "it must be a good pinch, a sincere effort."

"Got that, Sir Stanley?" asked the king. Sir Stanley nodded. "Good. Now give it yer best shot."

Sir Stanley did so and by so doing caused Eddie to yell "ouch" in pain. Since he was pinched in the rear end, it also caused Eddie to straighten up. Eddie banged his head upon the low ceiling and yelled out in pain again. While Eddie stood rubbing both ends, King Solomon laughed heartily.

"Well?" yelled Sherman.

"He felt it," yelled the king through fits of laughter.

"That settles it, then," said Sherman. "I'm afraid the lad is wide awake!"

That diagnosis stopped the king's laughter. Eddie looked around the room, all of the Sandmen looked terrified.

"Can Mortimer take the lad's imagination?" asked Sandy.

The king relayed his question to Sherman.

"If Mortimer can bring him into Dreamland wide awake, I have to believe he's capable of takin' his imagination as well. But that would be a different spell and I wouldn't know where to begin lookin' for it. But I must read you one important part." Sherman put his finger on the *Book of Spells* and cleared his throat. "To cast another spell on the person who has been brought into Dreamland wide awake with tainted sand, that person—the castee—must willin'ly join the witch castin' the spell—the caster; otherwise, the caster of the spell must wait until the castee can see the caster's castle before bein' allow to take the castee by force and then, still, the caster cannot cast another spell upon the castee until the exact instant before the castee's death in the Real World." Sherman looked up from the book. "What all that legal mumble-jumble means is that Mortimer cannot do anything to you until someone in the Real World attempts to wake you up. And since we have seven hours to the Real World's one, it means you have a full two to two and a half days, our time."

"It also explains why Mortimer didn't just take you," said Sandy. "He can't unless you can see his castle."

"And," said King Solomon, injecting his wisdom, "it means you must stay away from Dark Castle, his home."

"But what should I do?" asked Eddie, tears welling in his eyes. "I don't want to die."

King Solomon took pity on Eddie. "It seems I should think of somethin' else." In a confiding tone, he asked, "Can I think of somethin' else, Sir Stanley?"

"Me thinks that in a situation like this you would think of somethin' else."

"Me thinks so too," whispered the king, "but what?"

"I don't know what," said Sir Stanley.

"Me neither," said the king.

"Can I get back to sleep?"

King Solomon asked Sherman that question.

"Aye, he must get back to sleep. The Sandman who brought him here must throw some untainted sand into the lad' s eyes and that should do the trick."

"Mortimer cursed all the sand. How do I get meself some untainted sand?" asked Sandy to King Solomon, who relayed the question to Sherman.

"By undoin' the spell, of course," said Sherman. "But that would take a wizard."

"That's it!" said Sir Stanley. "That's what you'd probably suggest. But it is such a long shot. Still, it's probably the only shot we've got."

"Go on," said the king quietly, "what is it that I'd probably suggest?"

"I think you would suggest visitin' the great wizard, Beni."

"Would I?" Then loudly, "But, of course, Beni! I *would* think of that. Beni will know what to do. After all, there is no other good wizard in all of Dreamland."

"A wizard, all right!" said Eddie. He felt, at last, like he was getting help. "Where is this wizard?"

"Where?" Realization dawned on King Solomon's face. "Oh, Sir Stanley, I see why you called this a long shot. I'm afraid that visitin' Beni involves crossin' Dire Straits."

"And that's not all, yer highness," said Sir Stanley.

"Isn't that enough?," asked the king. "Ah, of course; you must go to the hidden city of Kyros and visit the Elfins. Kyros is at the top of Big Mountain, just across Dire Straits."

"The Elfins?" asked Eddie.

"Aye," said King Solomon, "and wonderful people they be, too. Of course, I haven't seen them for years."

Sir Stanley, noticing the look of confusion on Eddie's face, said, "Last we knew, Beni lived in Kyros with the Elfins."

"Oh," said Eddie.

"If you can make it to Kyros, then you will get help."

"That is such a dangerous journey," said Sandy, "but I see it must be made. If we can make it, surely Beni can help."

"Why does everyone keep saying if?" asked Eddie.

"'Tis not an easy task," said the king. "I'll be honest with you, no one has ever made it from here to there since Mortimer filled Dire Straits with sharks. I don't know if you know anything about sharks, but I'm warnin' you, they're deadly."

"We have sharks where I come from," said Eddie. "We can handle them."

"Splendid!" said the king. "Then I shall sendcha with two of me best chamberlains and with Sandy, of course."

"I won't leave his side," said Sandy. He understood his responsibility. "I'll make sure he gets back to the Real World, yer highness."

"Good," said the king. "Now, since time is of the essence, we must prepare for yer journey to Kyros. First things first, though; you will need a boat to cross Dire Straits."

6

DIRE
STRAITS

To Eddie's surprise, King Solomon proved to be an excellent organizer. In short order, a long procession marched toward the harbor. King Solomon rode in a sedan chair carried by eight chamberlains who struggled under the weight of the chair and of the king. The king had already arranged for a boat, forcibly volunteered two Sandmen—Shane and Safford—to accompany Eddie and Sandy, and ordered seven whole roasted pigs brought up from the storehouse. Seven groups of four chamberlains each carried a pig. Well-wishers and stragglers brought up the rear of the procession.

They reached a port which held many boats. Eddie could not see much of the water, for a thick fog hung over it. A lighter fog wove through the entire procession. The king ordered a halt in front of a wooden boat with one sail. Chamberlains loaded two strange looking contraptions through a door that led below deck. Foggy as it was, Eddie didn't see these contraptions clearly, so he asked Sandy what they were.

"Those are Mountain Climbers," said Sandy, "so that we may get up Big Mountain quickly. They are also designed to carry the pigs up the mountain; we wouldn't be able to get them up otherwise."

The chamberlains stowed away the seven roasted pigs last. They closed the hull door, securing it with a wooden bolt, then walked off the boat.

"Remember, lad, offer the pigs as a sign of friendship," King Solomon said. "Elfins are very reasonable creatures, if you bring them gifts of food. Dregs are the official gift takers for the Elfins, so give the pigs to the Dregs. Then you'll surely be treated well; otherwise, otherwise . . ."

The king left his sentence unfinished, but Eddie got the message. "Don't worry, your highness, I'll remember," Eddie assured the king. "I'll give the pigs to the Dregs."

"Remember, also, to watch out for the sharks of Dire Straits—they are deadly," said the king.

"Yer highness," said Sir Stanley, "don'tcha think you are forgettin' somethin'?"

"Am I?" said King Solomon. "If I am, I don't remember what it is that I'm forgettin'."

"Big Mountain, yer highness," prompted Sir Stanley.

"But Sir Stanley, I already told them they must climb Big Mountain to get to Kyros."

"The Trogs, yer highness," said Sir Stanley, "you should tell them about the Trogs."

"Should I?" asked King Solomon. "Oh, I suppose I must, but the lad might change his mind about goin'."

"No I won't. Why would I?"

"Well, lad," said the king, "once you cross Dire Straits, if you make it that far, you must climb Big Mountain before dark. Otherwise, the Trogs will getcha. And the Trogs are far worse than the sharks of Dire Straits."

"You see," said Sir Stanley, "mountains and cliffs, in Dreamland, have dangers of their own. They are inhabited by the worst of all beasts: Troglodytes—Trogs, for short. Trogs are cave-dwellin' creatures who cannot stand light and, therefore, only come out at night. So, if you make yer journey in daylight at least you can avoid them."

"And you must avoid them to reach Kyros, where the Elfins live," said King Solomon. "In that city, seek Princess Josefina.

Tell her I sentcha and she will undoubtedly take you to Beni."

"And, lad," said Sir Stanley, "you will find Princess Josefina at her Castle in the Air. Is all this clear?"

"Yes. Seek Princess Josefina at the Castle in the Air," Eddie said. "And avoid sharks and Trogs."

"Right. Now be off," said the king.

Eddie and Sandy hopped aboard the boat. The two volunteers, Shane and Safford, pushed the vessel away from the dock with two very large oars. All of those who had joined the king stood on the pier waving to Eddie.

The king in his booming voice yelled, "Good luck, er . . . uh . . . good luck, lad. Get back home safely and that's a royal command." To Sir Stanley he asked, "Can I make that a royal command?"

"Of course you can, yer majesty," said Sir Stanley, "for all the good it does."

"I thought so," said the king. It was, however, the last thing Eddie heard him say. And the last he saw of him, for the boat quickly entered the dense fog.

"I dislike good-byes so," said Sandy.

"You're not the only one," said Safford. "Given the choice, *I* certainly would have stayed."

"Now, now, Safford," said Shane, "we must obey a royal order cheerfully."

"Oh, I'm willin' to obey it, all right, but there's no way I'm gonna bear it cheerfully," said Safford in a tone that was anything but cheerful. "This order amounts to nothin' less than a death sentence."

"You really should show some manners in front of our Real World visitor," Shane told Safford. "Yer attitude reflects poorly on all of us."

"If he weren't here, we wouldn't be in this mess," Safford said. "So I don't see why I have to say nice things in front of him."

After an uncomfortable pause, Sandy said, "This journey is treacherous. We all realize that. You have to admit, though, that the fog is to our advantage."

"I don't have to admit anything," said Safford. "But I suppose you're right."

"Why is the fog to our advantage?" Eddie quietly asked Sandy.

"Because the sharks will have a harder time seein' us, that's all."

Eddie thought Sandy's observation strange, but remained quiet. For some time, the whole crew was silent. In the silence, Eddie thought of home. He thought of the ball game he had seen that night with his father. He thought of his baseball cards and pulled them out. While he flipped through them, the king's volunteers rowed through the fog. When Eddie looked up, the fog was so thick that he could barely see everyone on the deck, let alone the water.

"How long will it take us to cross Dire Straits?" Eddie asked as he put his cards back into his jacket pocket.

"Oh, no more than an hour," said Sandy. "Why, on a clear day you can see across Dire Straits to the other side. Quite an impressive sight then, with Big Mountain loomin' on the horizon."

No sooner had Sandy said this than the boat broke free from the fog. "Wow!" Eddie exclaimed. The view was as impressive as Sandy had described. Big Mountain was aptly named: even at this distance it required a left to right sweep of the head to take in its width and a skyward arch of the neck to see it disappear into the clouds above. Already, it looked close.

"Is it ever big!" said Eddie.

"Aye," said Sandy, who seemed preoccupied with other thoughts and wasn't even looking at Big Mountain. Instead, he stood with both hands on the wooden railing scanning the horizon all around the boat.

"What're you doing, Sandy?"

"I'm just lookin' out for sharks, that's all. Preferred it in the fog, I did. Out of the fog, I can see clearly . . . and clearly may not like what I see."

"Don't worry too much about sharks, Sandy. Me and my Dad went boating once and we saw a few sharks. It was no big deal really. Besides, my Dad said most sharks only eat plants."

"Not these sharks, they eat flesh," said Safford.

"Well, in the boat we'll be safe at any rate."

"Safe in this boat? Ha!" said Safford.

"I hope you're right, Eddie," Sandy said. "After all, you've seen sharks before and we've only heard tales about 'em."

"And tales can be greatly exaggerated," said Shane, giving Safford a meaningful glance.

"Look out!" shouted Sandy. "Sharks on the starboard side, closin' in on us!"

Eddie looked in the water. "Where?" He saw nothing.

"There!" Sandy pointed. But he did not point to the water. He pointed to the sky.

In the sky, Eddie saw a swarming gray mass. "What in the world are those things?"

"Those things are sharks," said Sandy.

"I thoughtcha saidcha saw sharks before," screamed Safford.

"Not like these sharks. These sharks are flying."

"But of course they're flyin'!" shouted Safford. "These are the flyin' sharks of Dire Straits."

"Flying sharks!" Eddie could not believe his eyes. Moving steadily towards the boat were a half dozen or so winged sharks. The sharks looked cumbersome as they slowly flew toward the boat. Suddenly, the lead shark dove into the water and the others followed.

"They've seen us!" shouted Sandy. "Now they'll move in swiftly."

Indeed, the fins sticking out of the water moved rapidly toward their boat. The two volunteers rowed with all their might, their eyes fixed on the shore, now about half a mile away. It was apparent, though, that the sharks would reach the boat before the boat would reach the shore.

"What are we going to do?" screamed Eddie.

"I was hopin' you'd know," cried Sandy.

"How dangerous are these things?"

"Deadly. They'll have us for lunch in no time. Soon they'll surface so that they can see us."

"You mean they can't see us underwater?" asked Eddie.

"No," said Sandy. "They move faster underwater, but they can only see when they're out of it."

"So they are swimming to where they think we will be?" asked Eddie.

"Sounds logical to me, lad," said Sandy.

"Then let's change direction."

The sharks had advanced to within a few hundred yards of the boat while Eddie and Sandy were yelling to each other. But Eddie's idea was readily accepted. Both of the king's men quickly slowed their pace and changed the angle of their approach toward Big Mountain. It worked! All of the fins passed in front of the boat, missing it by about thirty feet.

But it worked only temporarily, for first one shark, and then another, sprang out of the water. The first spotted the little boat and turned toward it. Each shark, in turn, emerged from the water, and flew at the boat. Soon, all seven of them (they were now close enough to count) closed in on the small vessel.

As they did, Eddie watched them. Each one was about fifteen feet long—half the size of the boat. Long, sawlike teeth filled their jaws. The sharks resembled the deadly great whites in all aspects except, of course, for the wings. The scaly wings extended a good three feet from either side of the creatures.

Soon, the first of the flying sharks reached the boat. It flew straight for Eddie.

"Duck!" screamed Sandy. Eddie instantly ducked. As he did so, the huge beast snapped its jaws where Eddie had stood. Instead of biting Eddie, however, the shark ripped through a piece of the wooden railing. Eddie was amazed—and terrified—by the ease with which the shark had bitten through the solid wood.

Three more sharks attacked the boat, each taking a chunk out of the boat's siding. One shark tore out the remainder of the railing above Eddie. Eddie now lay completely exposed on the deck as another shark came straight at him. Sandy saw it coming, raced towards Eddie and pulled him out of the way just as the shark's jaws closed over the deck where Eddie had been, rocking the boat. The hole left in the deck was half the size of Eddie.

Water began to flood the boat. Eddie realized that one way or another he and his friends were in trouble. At any moment, anyone of them could be eaten by the sharks. And if things continued as they were, the boat would soon sink and they'd all be eaten anyway. Something had to be done—and fast.

Eddie sprang to his feet and removed the wooden bar securing the hull doors which, left unsecured, swung open. Eddie stood with the bar in his hands awaiting the approach of a closing shark.

"Eddie, what are you doin'?" Sandy yelled.

"I'm trying something I saw in a movie," Eddie said. Just then the shark reached him and as it opened its jaws, he jammed the wooden

75

bar into the shark's mouth, forcing it to stay open. The shark turned and struggled as it flew through the air. Suddenly, the piece of wood gave way in the middle as the shark's jaws closed with a loud snap. The shark turned around in midair and lunged at Eddie. Eddie hit the deck beside Sandy, causing the shark to miss. It dove into the water, splashing both Sandy and Eddie.

"I guess it didn't work as well as in the movie," Sandy said consolingly, "but it was a brave effort, lad."

"Actually, it didn't work in the movie either, but I figured it was worth a try. Sandy, we've got to do something or we'll all be dead."

Shane, inspired by Eddie's bravery, jumped to his feet and grabbed a heavy oar. He began swinging it at an incoming shark. The shark merely bit it in half before it submerged beneath the waves.

Still the boat was a quarter of a mile from the shore. The sharks, sensing victory, intensified their assault. Safford dodged out of one's way as it bit the middle of the sail's post. The post teetered before it collapsed upon the deck, bringing the sail down with it. The sail covered Safford, who batted it around to find his way out.

One shark emerged from the water right in front of Eddie with its jaws wide open. Eddie saw its teeth coming down at him. But at that instant, another shark bit at the back of the boat, rocking it violently. Eddie was thrown backwards just out of the range of the closing jaws. He landed next to the opened hull door. Looking into the hull, he got another idea.

"The pigs!" Eddie yelled. "Help me with the pigs."

Sandy ran toward the door to help Eddie pull out a roasted pig. "Whatcha gonna do with it, lad?" he asked as they carried it to the edge of the deck. A flying shark approached them.

"At the count of three, toss it at the shark," Eddie said. "One . . . two . . . three!"

They heaved the pig with all their might. The shark went for the bait, snatching it between its jaws. Contented, it flew off with the hog in its mouth.

"Me goodness," shouted Sandy, "this may work."

The other Sandmen, also reaching that conclusion, grabbed a pig themselves. Eddie and Sandy went back for their second. Safford and Shane threw their hog and another winged shark dove for it. They rushed back for another pig.

Eddie and Sandy tossed their pig and again a shark snapped at it. Safford and Shane threw theirs as Eddie and Sandy got their third from the hull. Sandy grabbed the head, and Eddie the rear. Sandy backed towards the edge of the deck. Right then, a shark sprang out of the water and into the air between Sandy and Eddie. It snapped at the roasted pig, pulling it out of their arms. The shark swung its tailfins back and forth, hitting first Eddie and then Sandy. The fin felt like hard, slimy rubber as it hit Eddie's skin, knocking him backwards onto the deck. Sandy also fell backwards, plunging into Dire Straits.

The other Sandmen threw another hog. Then they hurried to get the last pig from the hull. Only one shark remained. But Eddie wasn't worrying about it: He was worrying about Sandy. Eddie peered over the deck where Sandy had gone overboard, but saw no sign of him.

The last shark circled the ship while Shane and Safford carried the final hog to the edge of the deck next to Eddie. Suddenly Sandy resurfaced. As he did, the shark spied him and headed seaward toward the little Sandman. Sandy gasped for breath and began swimming for the boat. The shark barreled down toward Sandy as the king's men heaved the last roasted pig in that direction. At the last second, the shark, rather than choosing Sandy, chose the pig. With the porker in its mouth, the winged beast flew off.

Eddie and the king's men helped pull Sandy aboard.

"That was much too close, I fear," said Sandy.

"We'd better get out of here before they come back," said Eddie.

The two volunteers got busy. Safford grabbed the one good oar left and began paddling for shore. Shane took the portion of the sail's post that had fallen to the deck and unfastened the sail. Then he used the post as an oar. In a matter of minutes, the boat—or what little of it that remained—reached the waves and was swept to shore. The exhausted crew found themselves safely at the foot of Big Mountain.

Eddie was glad to have gotten this far, but a disturbing thought hit him. "King Solomon said that the sharks of Dire Straits are bad. But he also said that the Trogs of Big Mountain are worse. Is that true?"

"Much worse, I'm afraid," said Sandy. "Our single consolation is that Trogs only come out in the dark. I believe that if we hurry we can make it to the top of Big Mountain before nightfall."

"Let's hope so," said Eddie. He felt like he needed to rest, but he realized that time was too precious to waste—especially if they were to make it up Big Mountain before dark.

7

BIG
MOUNTAIN

The Sandmen, recognizing the need for speed, unloaded the Mountain Climbers. Working together, they carried out one Climber and then the other. The Climbers, each about five feet tall, consisted of three separate but connected tracks. Eddie thought the tracks resembled those of military tanks he'd seen pictures of, except that these tracks were square and had hooks on them. Shane and Safford grabbed opposite ends of one device and pulled. To Eddie's surprise, one track extended about five feet from the center track. Extended, the device had two seats on one side of the center track. Below each seat were pedals, which were attached to a multitude of gears. The Sandmen placed the Climber at Big Mountain's steepest point. The Climber stayed there, as if suspended in air. So did the second Climber.

"Wow," said Eddie. "How do they stay up there?"

"The device is designed to climb up the face of a mountain," said Sandy. "The hooks on its tracks cling onto the mountain, keepin' it suspended. As you pedal, the tracks move and take you higher."

"Why, just get in it and we'll show you how it works," said Shane.

Shane strapped Eddie into his seat while Safford helped Sandy into the seat next to Eddie. As Eddie placed his feet onto the pedals, he looked between the other two tracks. Between them, he saw some compartments.

"What are those for?" he asked.

"Storage. Each of those would have carried a pig, if we still had them," said Shane.

"Which brings up another problem: We have no gifts for the Dregs to give to the Elfins," said Safford. "I don't think we should go at all."

"We have to, Safford," said Shane, "those are our orders."

"Yes, but King Solomon in all of his wisdom would not insist that we go up without the pigs. He was gracious enough to supply seven of them and stressed that they were gifts."

"And if it weren't for those pigs, we wouldn't have made it this far, Safford," said Sandy. "Surely the Elfins will understand that."

"I hope you're right," said Shane.

"I doubt if he is," said Safford. "I really don't think King Solomon would make us go, Shane."

"If you don't want to come, you don't have to," said Eddie.

"Right, I should just float back across Dire Straits on what's left of the boat," said Safford sarcastically. "I think I'd rather take me chances with you than tryin' to twice survive the flyin' sharks."

"If that's yer decision, then get in," said Shane as he strapped himself into the other Climber. Safford joined him. Shane turned to Eddie. "Now, let me explain how this works. You see the cylinder on yer side, lad?"

Eddie looked up by his track and over by Sandy's. Next to each track was a cylindrical object. Five clawlike hooks covered the outer end of the cylinder.

"That's yer Shooter, lad. See the lever near yer shoulder?"

Eddie nodded.

"Well, take aim and pull that lever. Like this." Shane pointed his Shooter straight up Big Mountain and pulled the lever. The clawlike hook, with a rope trailing it, shot out of the cylinder like a harpoon. The grapple hit the mountain, and Shane tugged at the attached rope. "See? Make sure it's good and secure."

Eddie took aim and fired. The grapple hit the mountain, but fell down. As it raced back down toward Eddie, a noise came from the Shooter; Eddie realized that the rope was being rewound automatically. In seconds, the grapple was ready to be shot again.

"Try again," Shane said.

The result was the same. Again he shot the grapple and again it bounced off the face of the mountain and came tumbling down.

"Don't get discouraged," said Sandy. "It takes a while to get the hang of it."

On his fourth try, the grapple held tight to the mountain when it hit.

"When we near the end of yer rope, I'll fire mine," said Sandy. "In that way, at least one grapple will be connected to the side of the mountain at all times."

"It's just an added precaution," said Shane, "in case all tracks slip at the same time—"

"Which has been known to happen," interrupted Safford.

"Thankye, Safford," said Shane. "But, believe me, 'tis a rare occurrence. Just remember to secure the ropes, for they may save yer life."

"Yes, sir," said Eddie, "I'll remember."

"Now, to go up or down, you merely pedal like a bicycle," Shane said. "Watch."

He and Safford pedaled their Mountain Climber. Its tracks rotated, clinging to Big

Mountain and moving up it. They back-pedaled and moved downward to rejoin Sandy and Eddie.

"Now you try it," Shane said.

Eddie and Sandy pedaled up a ways, then they pedaled back down.

"Wow!" said Eddie, "This is neat."

"Well, we better hurry, because we want to make it to the top before dark; if we don't, we won't make it at all—"

"The Troglodytes will make mincemeat of us," said Safford.

"How long before it gets dark?" asked Eddie.

"About four hours," said Shane, "give or take fifteen minutes."

"How long will it take us to get to the top?" Eddie asked.

"About four hours."

"Give or take fifteen minutes," said Safford.

Realizing they had little or no time to spare, the two pairs began their ascent in earnest. Eddie's rope automatically rewound as he and Sandy neared it. When there were within ten feet of Eddie's grapple, Sandy shot the one on his side. He gave the rope a tug to make sure it was secure. As they neared Sandy's, Eddie aimed and fire his grapple again. This time it took just two tries to secure it. Alternatively shooting their grapples while pedaling, they rose up the face of Big Mountain.

Eddie was enjoying himself. Climbing Big Mountain in a Mountain Climber gave Eddie a great sensation. It felt like gliding up the side of a cliff. The tracks bent with the contours of the steep mountain. Eddie's suspended seat flowed perfectly with the Climber. He look down to watch the shore shrink smaller and smaller; he looked up to see the clouds high above grow bigger and bigger.

After two hours of climbing, though, Eddie had changed his tune. He was exhausted: Pedaling constantly up the side of this huge mountain was hard work. Also, it sometimes took several tries before the hook on the rope would catch. At best, it was a tedious process—and one Eddie could see no end to. Looking up, all he saw was mountain until it disappeared into the clouds. Looking down, he could see that they had climbed up so far that looking down was too scary.

Finally, he could take no more, "How much farther do we have to go?"

"Oh, another hour, hour and a half, I should imagine," Sandy said.

"Just keep pedalin' and we'll get there," said Safford.

Eddie looked up. Thoughts of home kept him pedaling. He hoped with all his heart that

Beni, the great wizard, would get him back home quickly.

Suddenly, that which had been known to happen happened. The Climber that Sandy and Eddie rode in slipped simultaneously on all three tracks, dragging a little gravel for a foot or two. Then it came completely loose and fell rapidly downward. Eddie and Sandy both let out a scream as the Climber fell free from the mountain. Eddie spun in circles as the Climber headed down, but the Shooter stayed upright as it rotated on its own wheel. As the rope on Sandy's side became taut, the Climber snapped and bounced, hanging precariously by that rope three feet from the face of Big Mountain. It dangled and swayed there at an angle which had Eddie facing downward. They were so high up that Eddie immediately closed his eyes, not wanting to look down.

"Hang on!" Shane's voice echoed down to them.

Shane and Safford began descending to where Sandy and Eddie's Climber hung. They pulled to a stop on Eddie's side of the Climber.

"Hit the release button for yer rope, lad," Shane said.

"And open yer eyes," Safford said.

Eddie followed the second direction first; then finding the release button, he pushed it. "Now, slowly rotate the cylinder toward you.

But I'm warnin' you that the hook will drop toward you so put yer hand over it." While Eddie did this, Shane unstrapped himself and climbed up the track. "Good. Now toss the hook toward me." He reached over as Eddie tossed the grapple to him. Shane climbed back into his seat with Eddie's rope in his hands. "Now hold on."

Shane and Safford pedaled up, using Eddie's rope to straightened out the dangling Climber. When it was straight, they guided it back toward the mountain. It hit the mountain and bounced off the side. Again, it hit and bounced. On its third impact it stuck.

"Now pedal," said Shane.

Eddie and Sandy obeyed. Slowly the Climber moved; then it regained its sure and steady ascent. Eddie, though, was now less sure of it and grew steadily less fond of it. As they neared the spot were they had slipped, Eddie held his breath. When they made it past that point without incident, he sighed with relief.

"Ok, lad, hit yer release again." Eddie did, and this time the rope rewound.

"How much longer?" Eddie asked.

"We'll be lucky to make it at all after that little mishap," Safford said.

Eddie understood Safford's meaning: The fall had wasted about fifteen minutes and, give or take, that was all the spare time they had.

Soon the travelers entered the clouds. It was like the fog of Dire Straits only whiter. Another ten minutes and they rose above them, the clouds laying like a blanket of snow below.

Eddie noticed that the sky had grown darker. "How much longer now?"

"Not very much longer, luckily," said Sandy.

"Not very much longer and the Trogs will come out of their caves," said Safford.

Eddie looked at the face of Big Mountain. Here and there he saw patches of snow. But he also saw caves—and lots of them. Trogs, cave-dwelling creatures by day, would soon come out. Eddie didn't want to be anywhere near them when they did. He forced his aching legs to move faster.

Up into another cloud the foursome headed. Somewhere in the middle of it the Mountain Climbers suddenly stopped and would go no farther.

"We have come as far as the Climbers will take us," said Shane. "We must continue our journey on foot."

They unstrapped themselves and hopped off the Climbers onto a ledge. The mountain here was not steep, which was one reason the Mountain Climbers had stopped. As Eddie walked he heard the crunch of snow beneath his feet. Gradually the slope of the mountain became more level.

"We don't have much farther to go now," said Shane.

Eddie was glad of that, for dusk was now changing into night.

Within minutes it was completely dark. In that darkness, the group continued on through the cloud, somewhere near the top of Big Mountain.

A loud shriek interrupted the silence of the night. And what an unearthly shriek it was. It sent shivers through Eddie's spine.

"What was that?" he asked, fearing that he already knew. He did.

"It's a Trog, of course," said Safford. "Now we're all doomed."

They heard a scraping, crunching sound as the hooks on the tracks of their Mountain Climbers were ripped from the mountain. Another high-pitched shriek followed. Then they heard the sound of the Climbers banging repeatedly against the mountain, more distant each time.

"They've thrown our Climbers down the mountain," whispered Sandy. "Now we really must hurry."

Eddie, Shane and Safford needed no further coaxing. They began running.

"Wait for me!" yelled Sandy as he tried to catch up.

They ran for five minutes nonstop before they slowed to a jog.

"Do you think we've lost them?" asked Eddie.

"I don't know," said Sandy.

They could only see about eight to ten feet in either direction (after all, they were running through a cloud and it was dark).

Suddenly they heard another loud shriek. And it sounded near. Once more the four began to run. Soon they reached a fork in the path.

"Which way do we go?" asked Eddie.

"I don't remember," said Shane.

"Great," Safford said. "Here we are bein' chased by Trogs andcha don't remember which way to go!"

A growl came from behind them and all four screamed. Turning toward the dark mist behind them, Eddie saw the black silhouette of a Trog! It walked on hoofed feet with legs like horses, except that a Trog had only two legs. On its head were two ramlike horns. Its arms were as thick as a gorilla's and on its hands were long sharp claws. All in all, the Trog's profile was devilish. It took a step toward them. Eddie decided it was no time to be standing around.

"Quick, this way!" he called, pointing to and running toward the left path.

His three friends followed without hesitation. So did the unfriendly Trog, but it walked. Soon they could not see it behind them. In front of them they saw a distant light.

"The city lights of Kyros!" yelled Shane. "Run for them."

Behind, Eddie heard the Trog's pace quicken. The sound came closer—the Trog was gaining on Eddie and his friends as they ran desperately toward the lights. Suddenly the Trog's silhouette came back in view.

The lights, near and bright, gave Eddie hope; he raced for them. He burst through the cloud first, seeing the lights of Kyros. His three friends came clear of the cloud right on Eddie's heels. The Trog did not come through it. Instead, it stopped just within the cloud and shrieked as it covered its eyes. It backed away from the lights. Then it turned and ran.

"We made it! We made it!" shouted Safford with glee. "I don't believe it, we made it!"

Safford dropped to the ground and kissed it. The others laughed. They were relieved by their timely arrival at Kyros. Now, Eddie thought, all we have to do is find Princess Josefina. The princess will take us to Beni; Beni will cast a spell and I'll be home. He honestly thought it would be as simple as that. But Eddie was forgetting one small detail. Eddie was forgetting that he and the Sandmen had no gifts.

8

NO GIFTS!

Eddie took a look at Kyros. "Wow," he exclaimed. Kyros seemed to float completely above the cloud which, instead of obscuring Kyros, surrounded it. The cloud and the city reflected like one big bright white glow. The cloud surrounding Kyros was white; the snow blanketing Kyros was white; even the streets were white. The buildings were not white, but the lights twinkled off them as if they were made of crystal. Their elegant design, though more modern than the buildings of Sandadu, maintained an old-fashioned appeal. The city's streets, paved with white tar, were wide and well lighted.

The most remarkable sight in all of Kyros, its castle, was at the highest point of the city, resting on a small cloud of its own. Under this cloud was a rainbow, which because of all the lights was visible even at night.

Sandy pointed to it and said, "There's the Castle in the Air. That's where we'll find Princess Josefina."

"Then what are we waitin' for?" said Shane. "Let's be off."

After they had gone a couple of blocks, two strange creatures with doglike features stepped in front of them.

Eddie looked at the two creatures with bulldog faces. They were each covered with tan fur. They wore leather skirts and held long, carved spears. One held up a hand, and said, "Halt!" The palm of its hands had dark brown pads on it, like those on the paws of a dog.

"Who are they?" Eddie whispered to Sandy.

"They are Dregs," Sandy whispered back, "the gift collectors for the Elfins."

One of the Dregs spoke, "Give us gifts for Elfins."

"We don't have any gifts," said Eddie, "you see, we had some but we lost them when we—"

"WHAT?" shouted the Dreg. "NO GIFTS?"

"Sir," said Shane, "what the lad means is that we are under instructions to give our gifts directly to Princess Josefina."

"No! Give us gifts now or you no see princess," the Dreg said in his deep, rough voice.

"I knew this was a bad idea," said Safford. Shane hushed him and tried again.

"Our gift is of a personal nature and we cannot give it to anyone but the princess."

"Me no like sound of this. Me think boy told truth and you no gifts." Turning to the other Dreg, he said, "Take 'em 'way!" The Dreg took a step toward them.

"Wait!" Sandy said. The Dreg stopped. "Our gift is a visitor from the Real World. Eddie is his name."

"Hi, sir," said Eddie. "I must see the princess."

"You no see princess. You no good as gift. Gifts must be good. Roasted pig is favorite. Taste yummy." The Dreg patted his stomach and licked his chops.

"We had seven," Eddie said.

" 'Tis, true, that," said Safford. "But the boy insisted on throwin' them to the sharks."

"Safford! I am appalled," said Shane. "Remember yerself. We had to feed them to the flyin' sharks to make it across Dire Straits."

"Unfortunate for you," the Dreg said. "Take 'em 'way, Oscar!"

The Dreg called Oscar stepped forward and clasped shackles around the wrists of the four visitors, chaining them all together. Then he said, "Come!" and tugged at their chains to lead them forward. He led them down an alley, stopping at the last building. A sign above the door read "Dungeon."

"Lock them up!" said the Dreg who seemed to be in charge.

"Yes, sir," said Oscar.

"Don't we get a trial?" asked Eddie.

The first Dreg laughed heartily. "Boy come to Kyros with no gifts and want night trial."

"The boy does not want a night trial," Shane said, shaking his head.

"He do so," said the Dreg.

"He does not," said all three Sandmen together.

"But he do," said the Dreg, "he say he do, so he do. We arrange trial and find you guilty immediately."

"That doesn't sound like a fair trial," said Eddie.

"You want trial and expect fair one, too?" said the Dreg in disbelief. Both Dregs laughed. "No gifts, you guilty. Simple as that. Punishment simple, too. We chain you outside town, in dark cloud. Then we let Trogs carry out punishment. Next morning, all gone." Both laughed even harder than before.

Eddie, however, was horrified. "Why, that's awful punishment."

"Awful not bring gifts. Should know better."

95

"We did bring gifts, I told you that already," Eddie said. "They were eaten by the sharks."

"Better if you been eaten by sharks than come to Kyros with no gifts. Now you be eaten by Trogs. Lock them up! Enough of boy for now. We arrange trial within hour, find you guilty."

Oscar opened a big wooden door and dragged Eddie and the three Sandmen down a long, dark staircase. At the bottom of the stairs were a number of prison cells. The Dreg opened one and pushed the four inside. He locked the door shut.

"Tonight we feed you to Trogs," he said. They heard him chuckle as he walked away.

"I don't like these Dregs," Eddie said.

"No one does," said Safford. "But don't say I didn't warn you about comin' to Kyros without gifts."

"Dregs are horrible. If the Elfins have Dregs collect gifts for them, they must be horrible, too. How did we expect them to help us? I want to go home." It was all too much for Eddie. He began to cry. "I miss my mom and dad."

"Don't worry, lad," said Sandy, patting Eddie on the shoulder. "Somehow we'll get out of this mess. The Elfins aren't at all horrible, really."

The four stayed huddled together in their small cell. Except for a flat plank, which served as a bed, the room was bare. Rats scurried across the floor of this and other cells where other prisoners, all Dregs, were kept. One of these prisoners, an ugly Dreg with one white eye and one brown eye, asked what Eddie and his friends were in for. When they told him they were arrested for not bringing gifts, he laughed and said, "We not see much of you then. Nice meeting you and good-bye." The other prisoners found his remarks amusing and laughed as well.

Although Eddie was in no laughing mood, the hour passed quickly. Oscar returned with orders to take the four prisoners out of their cell. The Dreg unlocked the door and again yanked at the chain to drag them out. He led them upstairs where the bossy Dreg waited.

"The boy who want night trial get night trial," said the waiting Dreg. "Judge ready now. Come."

He led the group through a door, down a hall and into a courtroom. "Stay," he ordered.

He then nodded to a Dreg who was already in the courtroom. This Dreg said, "Honorable Judge Cody presiding."

Judge Cody entered at his cue. He was also a Dreg, but unlike the others, he wore a black robe and black spectacles. Judge Cody sat behind the enormous desk in front of the courtroom.

"Let we get this over with," said Judge Cody. "I just ready eat dinner when you called me, Grover. Now what this all 'bout?"

"Boy and Sandmen have no gifts for Elfins," Grover said.

"That true?" the judge asked of Eddie.

"Well, sir, we brought gifts, but—"

"Asked 'yes' or 'no' question, young man," Judge Cody said, "and I 'preciate 'yes' or 'no' answer. Do you have gifts for Elfins?"

"No, sir," said Eddie, dejectedly.

"Guilty as charged," said Judge Cody, pounding his gavel on his desk. "Case closed. Punishment immediate. Leave for Trogs."

"But, sir, if you would let me explain—"

Judge Cody interrupted, "You admit you have no gifts, you guilty as charged. Need no explanations. Now if you 'scuse me, I go home eat dinner. Leave 'em for Trogs."

"Wait, sir," said Safford. "I demand a separate trial."

"Safford, you should be ashamed of yerself," said Shane.

"Well, I'm not. I want me own trial."

"Okay," said Judge Cody. "Speak."

"In the mornin' would be fine, yer honor."

"We do it now," said Judge Cody. "Come with boy, did you?"

"Well, sure, but—"

"Guilty. Take 'em all 'way, Grover."

"But, but," Safford said.

Judge Cody ignored him, stood up and left the courtroom. Grover grabbed a torch and ordered Oscar to bring the prisoners. Oscar pulled Eddie and the Sandmen out of the courtroom, into the alley, and back down the street where they had entered Kyros. All the way Safford complained about his miserable fate. Grover, torch in hand, led them into the darkness of the cloud. Just out of view of the city lights, he stopped. There was a tree with chains driven into the ground near it. Oscar strapped Eddie and each Sandman to those chains.

"This teach you. Bring gifts next time," said Grover.

"I can't see as there will be a next time," said Safford, "since you're leavin' us for the Trogs."

"Oh, right," said Grover. "Never mind 'bout next time. Good-bye, stupid visitors with no gifts."

Then he and Oscar left, taking the torch with them. Eddie and his friends found themselves in total darkness, left to the mercy of the Trogs.

"This is all the boy's fault," said Safford.

"I'm sorry," said Eddie. "I really am. I had no idea this would happen."

"Don't worry about it, lad," said Sandy. "It could've happened to any of us."

"Or all of us," said Safford. "Like it did."

"Hush," said Shane, whispering, "do you want to attract the Trogs?"

Just then, a terrible shriek rose from the distance and all four chained prisoners jumped.

"Didcha hear that?" said Sandy.

"Of course we heard that," said Safford. "Do you think we're deaf."

"Quiet, please," said Shane. "If we just sit here, maybe we'll still be here in the mornin'."

But after he said this, footsteps could be heard in the distance, fast footsteps.

"We're in for it now," said Safford.

Six figures came into view, walking quickly. But they were not Trogs. Each held a torch and was covered head to toe by a dark robe. The figures approached Eddie and the Sandmen, took out keys and unlocked the chains.

"Come with us," said a soft voice. It was the first female voice Eddie had heard in Dreamland. He thought of his mother and longed for home.

"Who are you?" asked Eddie.

"Hush, now," said the voice. "When it is safe we will speak. Follow us."

She put out her hand and Eddie took it. He was confused; he wondered how anyone other than the Dregs knew they were chained there—or had keys to release them. A dozen questions jumped to his mind, but he followed in silence nonetheless. The six robed figures, the three Sandmen and Eddie made their way to Kyros.

Once inside the city, the person who held Eddie's hand spoke again. "You may ask your questions now, Eddie."

Eddie's eyes grew wide. "How did you know my name?"

"I know who you are and why you came."

"But how do you know? And who are you?" asked Eddie.

"Aye," said Sandy, "who, indeed?"

The six women laughed gleefully. The one who spoke pushed back her hood. In unison, Shane and Safford said, "Princess Josefina!"

The princess merely smiled. Eddie liked her smile; it was warm. He took a good look at her. She had shoulder-length brown hair and deep blue eyes. Although she was a petite lady, her eyes revealed a powerful presence. Eddie felt he could trust her.

"Wow," he said softly. "Pleased to meet you, Princess Josefina."

"The pleasure is all mine," said Princess Josefina. "These are helpers of mine, other Elfins."

The other Elfins also pushed back their hoods. Each one was beautiful, though none more so than the princess herself. A couple had boyish hairstyles and Eddie noticed their ears were pointed. He idly wondered if the princess's were as well. As if in answer to his thoughts, she brushed her hair behind her ear. It, too, was pointed.

"But how do you know about me?" asked Eddie.

"The omens forewarned me," said the princess. Then she closed her eyes and quoted:

> *A boy not from this land of ours shall bring*
> *No gifts; though gifts he had–prepared by a king*
> *Who sent him hither seeking help. The boy's*
> *Own future mirrors ours. We have the choice:*
> *Refuse to help and share his fate. Or give aid*
> *And hope what evil made can be unmade . . .*

She opened her eyes. "That is it, but that is enough. I prefer to unmake the evil Mortimer made. Now, let's go to my castle. You could use a good night's sleep."

"But, yer highness," said Sandy, "the lad's time—"

"Is limited," said the princess.

"Those were me very words," said Sandy, shocked.

"I know," said the princess. "I know, also, that there is time enough for sleep. Eddie, how many hours do you usually sleep at night?"

"Well, I usually go to bed at eight or nine and sleep till six or seven. But tomorrow's Saturday, so I'd sleep in."

"Fine. You have been not quite one day in Dreamland. Roughly three hours your time. Safely, four or five hours more remain. Another day or day and a half, our time. Time enough for sleep. With a fresh start in the morning, success will come more readily."

"Sounds logical," said Sandy.

"I'm glad you think so," said Princess Josefina, smiling.

"But can't you just take us to Beni?" asked Eddie. "I want to go home."

"I know," said Princess Josefina, "but we'll discuss it in the morning." She then bid them to follow her to the Castle in the Air.

9

CASTLE
IN THE AIR

"Thank you for saving us, your highness," said Eddie as they walked toward the Castle in the Air. He and the princess walked ahead of the rest of the group. He wanted to be polite before he asked a question that might appear rude: "I was wondering—"

"You were wondering about the Dregs. Why we Elfins have them collect gifts and punish those who don't bring gifts."

Eddie nodded; her words captured his thoughts better than his would have.

"Well," said Princess Josefina, "what I'm about to tell you is a secret. Can you keep a secret?"

"Oh, yes."

"Good," she said. "You see, the gifts are not for us. We have never required gifts—or hired Dregs. The Dregs appointed themselves gift-takers and keep the gifts themselves."

"Why do you let them do that?" Eddie asked.

"Because we see no harm in it. Besides, it keeps unwanted visitors away. Anyway, the Dregs won't actually hurt anyone. Their bark is worse than their bite."

"But they left us out in the dark for Trogs to eat."

"And we freed you. Just as we free all the unfortunate who come without gifts. The Dregs never find out. They think their victims have been eaten."

Eddie smiled.

"I sense your feelings about us have improved," the princess said.

Soon they stood just outside the small cloud with the rainbow under it, looking at the Castle in the Air. They entered the cloud and began walking up through the rainbow. (Trying to catch a rainbow in the Real World is impossible; not so in Dreamland.) Eddie watched the colors reflect off his skin. "Wow!" he said. He stuck his arm out from the red into the orange range, and his arm become both colors at once. He kept changing as he went from one color to the next. For the life of him, he was certain his feet were touching nothing but the cloud itself. At the top of the cloud, the Castle in the Air rocked gently with the wind, floating on the cloud like a boat on the water. The breeze made Eddie shiver.

"I see why you call it the Castle in the Air," said Eddie. Everything in Dreamland seemed to fit its name.

"Everyone builds their own castles in the air," said the princess, "but to my knowledge ours is the only real one. It's also the only castle made of ice."

"Ice? It's made of ice?" Eddie asked. "But ice melts."

"I know," said the princess. "And you're thinking that's a terrible weakness for a castle to have. But you're forgetting that when ice melts it turns to water—and Mortimer stays far away from water. So that supposed weakness is our castle's greatest strength."

"I didn't think of that." Eddie had to admit that building a castle out of ice seemed like a more brilliant defense than building one of sand. He looked at the glistening palace with renewed interest. It loomed like a giant ice sculpture—perfectly shaped right down to the finest detail.

Princess Josefina led them into the castle. Although made of ice, its interior was

pleasantly warm. So warm that Princess Josefina and the other Elfins removed their heavy robes. Under the robe, Princess Josefina wore a flowing white outfit made of fine, lacy material that accentuated her beauty. She dismissed the other Elfins. Then she led Eddie, Sandy, Shane, and Safford down an icy corridor. The ice did occasionally produce a drip from the ceiling—another hindrance for Mortimer, thought Eddie. He was also struck by another difference between Sand Castle and Castle in the Air. At Sand Castle, there were Sandmen everywhere; here he saw no Elfins other than the ones who had entered the castle with him.

"We don't feel the need here for the tight security they have on Sandsibar," said Princess Josefina, as if in answer to his thoughts. "Mortimer hasn't appeared here in centuries." The princess opened a door to a large bedroom. "You will stay here tonight. Sleep well, gentlemen. I'll see you in the morning."

Eddie hit the cozy bed, his head sinking into the down pillows. He was more tired than he could ever remember being, but he couldn't sleep. Try as he might, sleep would not come. His first day in Dreamland had been exciting, exhilarating and exhausting. But despite being thoroughly tired, his first night was sleepless.

Unable to sleep—even in a room full of
Sandmen—Eddie got out of bed at dawn. He
began thumbing through his baseball cards,
one by one, gazing a little longer at Joe Ortiz's.
Hearing someone approach, he pocketed
them. A moment later Princess Josefina
entered the room.

"Did you sleep well?" she asked.

"Well, actually, I didn't sleep at all,"
Eddie said.

"Then you are wide awake," she said as
her eyes grew very wide indeed.

"Didn't you know that?" asked Eddie.

Princess Josefina laughed, "I don't know
everything. I certainly sensed it, but I was
hoping I was wrong. Mortimer's magic is very
powerful. I do know that. I also know that you
must leave immediately after breakfast."

"You'll take me to Beni after breakfast?"

"Not exactly, no. Help me wake your
friends. Gentlemen, time to eat!"

Eddie shook Sandy, while the princess
tapped Shane and Safford. The Sandmen rose
reluctantly and groggily from their beds. (It
should come as no surprise that Sandmen love
their sleep.)

Once they were up, Princess Josefina took
Eddie's hand and they walked down the icy
corridor, followed by the Sandmen. They
entered a large eating area. Many Elfins were

already eating, and when the princess entered they all stood.

"Good morning," said the princess. "This is Eddie. King Solomon, in his wisdom, has sent us Eddie, a Real World visitor. Mortimer has cast an evil spell upon him and he is in danger. He must make it to Beni, today. So, prepare the elevators. They must be ready by the time our visitors are finished with breakfast. Go now, and hurry."

Immediately, dozens of Elfins rushed out of the room.

Princess Josefina led Eddie and the Sandmen to the food line. Eddie had pancakes with lots of syrup.

"Does Beni live in the castle?" asked Eddie.

"No," said the princess.

"Don't worry, lad," said Sandy, "Kyros isn't that large of a city. It won't take long to reach Beni regardless of which part of town we have to visit."

"Beni doesn't live in Kyros anymore," said the princess.

"What?" Sandy asked.

"I'm afraid you have a long journey ahead of you today."

"A long journey?" Sandy looked sullen.

"Beni now lives a good eight hours' walk from here."

"Do you know where?" asked Eddie.

"Oh, yes," said the princess. "I know, more or less. Now, which of you brought Eddie to Dreamland?"

"I did, yer highness," said Sandy.

"Then you alone need accompany him. Beni dislikes crowds."

"Fine with me," said Safford.

"How will you guys get back?" Eddie asked, fearing that Shane and Safford would have to cross Dire Straits once more.

"Don'tcha worry about us, lad," said Shane. "We are Sandmen after all. In less than one week our time, it will be night again in the Real World. We'll merely enter it from here. When we return from the Real World we'll return straight to Sandsibar. So, have no worries for us, lad. 'Tis you that we worry about. Right, Safford?" When Safford didn't answer, Shane asked again, "Safford?"

"Oh, all right," said Safford, "we will certainly, most assertively, absolutely, positively worry aboutcha, lad. Good enough?"

"That's fine," said Shane, "but next time say it like you mean it."

"I mean it," said Safford. "I mean I really, really mean it." Changing his tone, he added, "I guess I do owe the little fella some thanks for savin' me life."

"Better," said Shane. "I also would like to thank you for gettin' us past the sharks, lad."

111

"You're welcome," said Eddie, "but I saved myself, too, you know."

"It is time," said Princess Josefina. Eddie said good-bye to Safford and Shane. Then he and Sandy left with the princess. Wanting to make sure that Eddie and Sandy had enough food, she stopped in the kitchen and had the cook prepare a care package for them. Then she led them outside the palace. The wind hit Eddie with an arctic chill, but fortunately he wore his jacket. Once more, Eddie walked incredulously upon the cloud and through the rainbow.

The princess led them east through the snow-lined streets of Kyros. In the daylight, Kyros was more beautiful than at night. Sunlight danced off, through and around the crystal-like buildings, making the whole city beam. Kyros emanated energy and felt alive. The feeling was contagious; Eddie, despite his lack of sleep, caught it and felt rejuvenated.

At the eastern side of Big Mountain, they reached the elevators that the Elfins had rushed to prepare.

"The elevators are the quickest and safest way up and down Big Mountain," Princess Josefina said. "I will ride down a little ways with you and show you where to look for Beni."

Eddie, Sandy and Princess Josefina got on what the Elfins called an "elevator." It looked more like a window cleaner's platform, consisting of a flat board enclosed by metal rails which attached to the poles at each corner. The elevator was hooked up to a pulley system. Elfins operated the pulleys, lowering the elevator into the cloud. When it came out of the cloud, it stopped. Eddie, Sandy and Princess Josefina got off it and onto another. The princess told them a whole series of elevators were set up, reaching from the top of Big Mountain to the bottom. As each elevator stopped, a group of Elfins stood ready to work the pulleys of the next. The group entered and exited cloud number two.

"When you reach the bottom of Big Mountain, you will see a river," said Princess Josefina as the elevator dipped into a third cloud.

"Aye," said Sandy, "I'm familiar with it. Poisoned River."

"Is the river poisoned?" asked Eddie.

"It is," said Princess Josefina with a nod. "Mortimer, finding water of no use to him, sought to make it of no use to anyone else, so don't drink the water. There is, however, a greater danger than the water."

"Aye," said Sandy, "the Water Bugs."

The princess nodded, "Those, too. But I was referring to Giants."

Sandy gasped. "I had completely forgotten that the river ran through the Valley of Giants. Isn't there another route?"

The princess shook her head.

"I do so hate the idea of runnin' into Giants," said Sandy.

The elevator came out of the third cloud, revealing the breathtaking view below them. "Wow!" said Eddie. Far below, Eddie saw a river winding through a beautiful valley. He knew it must be Poisoned River and that the valley must be the Valley of Giants. He had never been to the Valley of Giants before; but he had been to Yosemite Valley in California. This valley reminded him of Yosemite—serene and majestic, at least from this vantage point.

Eddie also saw that the Elfins had chosen to install their elevators at Big Mountain's most vertical point. He could make out a whole series of elevators below him: There must be hundreds and hundreds of them, he thought. (Actually there were only one hundred and forty-seven of them.) Big Mountain spread out like a crescent around the elevators; yet, despite the immensity of the semi-circle, it made up only a small portion of the eastern side of Big Mountain. Poisoned River began beyond the slope to their right.

Princess Josefina pointed to that ribbon of water. "At the river's end, you will find Beni."

"At the river's end?" Eddie looked down. He could not see its end, but he didn't see it continue beyond the valley. At the horizon the landscape grew more desolate, with no water at all in view. "How far is that?"

"Far enough," said the princess.

"And how will we know when we get there?" Eddie asked.

"You will know," said the princess. They got off this elevator; Sandy and Eddie got on the next. "I must leave you now," said Princess Josefina. She kissed Sandy on the forehead, making his face turn bright red.

"Gosh," he said, removing his cap and holding it in his hands.

"Good luck," said the princess. "Take good care of the boy. I wish I could have helped more."

"You have done enough, Princess Josefina," said a truly flattered Sandy.

"Time will tell if that is true," Princess Josefina said. Then she kissed Eddie on the forehead. "May you have a safe and successful journey. All of Dreamland awaits your final fate. If Mortimer is successful in stealing your imagination, we shall all be doomed by the things he'll dream up. So, good luck, Eddie, and God bless you."

"Don't worry, your highness," said Eddie, "Mortimer won't get my imagination."

The princess smiled. "I like your emotion. It's filled with hope and optimism. You will need both to beat the odds and return safely home."

"I can't wait to get home," said Eddie, "and tell my parents about this." He paused, thinking. "Boy, are they going to have a hard time believing this one."

Princess Josefina laughed. "It does not matter what your parents will or will not believe. What matters is that you return and have the chance to tell them. What matters is that you believe. I sense you do. Hang on to that belief: It can save you. Never give up hope."

"I won't," said Eddie.

She kissed Eddie again, this time on the cheek. Then the primitive elevator began to descend. Eddie looked up and waved at Princess Josefina. When the elevator stopped, he and Sandy got onto the next one. The group of Elfins waiting there began pulling on the ropes to lower them. Eddie watched the smiling face of Princess Josefina until he could no longer see it. Then he looked down at the river below them. He wondered what lay ahead of them. How long would it take to get to Beni? Could they avoid the dangers along Poisoned River?

10

POISONED
RIVER

Eddie and Sandy reached the one
hundred forty-seventh—and last—elevator
about two hours later. The elevator touched
down at the foot of Big Mountain without
Eddie giving it any thought at all that it had
taken less than half the time to go down the
mountain as it had to go up.

Eddie and Sandy began walking in the
direction of Poisoned River. Eddie was sure
Beni could help him; that is, if he could make it
to Beni. But he was worried about Water Bugs
and Giants.

"How bad are Water Bugs?" he asked.

"Deadly," said Sandy. "They're the only
livin' creatures that have adapted to Poisoned
River. Livin' as long as they have in it, they

are themselves poisonous. So don't get near 'em, lad."

"Oh, I won't," said Eddie. "What do they look like?"

"In the river they look like rocks, but they move."

"How big are they?"

"Oh, I should say that a full-grown Water Bug is about six inches long. So not very big as far as things go."

"But huge as far as bugs go," said Eddie.

Sandy nodded. "Aye. And I should warn you: They're very strong and durable bugs. They've been known to leap several feet through the air, and try as you might to crunch them, they survive."

"Can we avoid them?"

"Aye, lad, if we keep our eyes peeled."

Eddie didn't like the sound of these bugs, and he hoped he wouldn't have to meet them face to face.

"And what about the Giants?" Eddie asked as he and Sandy neared the right slope of the crescent they had descended into.

"Giants are the most disagreeable of all people in Dreamland," said Sandy, looking very disagreeable himself as he pondered the behemoths. "They're quick to anger and equally quick to smash intruders to bits, which is relatively easy for them to do. To me way of thinkin', they are far worse than Water Bugs."

"Can you at least talk to them?" asked Eddie.

"Well, certainly, if you mean can they talk. You wouldn't want to talk to them, though," Sandy said, shaking his head.

"Why not? They wouldn't smash us to bits before we could talk to them, would they?"

"Personally, I wouldn't wait to find out. I'd be runnin' as fast as I could in the opposite direction."

"They're that strong?"

"Stronger," said Sandy. "Besides, lad, they carry huge clubs to clobber things with. We definitely want to stay away from both Water Bugs and Giants."

"Well, I hope we do," said Eddie. And he sincerely meant it. He didn't want anything else to stand in the way of finding Beni and getting home. Even the prospect of starting on his science project thrilled him more at this point than the thought of facing more Dreamland monsters—flying sharks and Trogs had been enough.

For some time they had heard the sound of rushing water; soon they rounded the large slope and angled for the river, which they could now see as well.

"Wow!" said Eddie as they neared the river. He could see where it sprang from the side of Big Mountain in one continual gush.

When they reached Poisoned River, it was still early in the day. Eddie looked at and into the river. It looked perfectly normal to him and he said so to Sandy.

"Aye, but looks can be deceivin', lad. There's absolutely nothin' normal about this river. So let's be careful, shall we?"

Eddie and Sandy made their way along the banks of Poisoned River, ever watchful for Water Bugs.

"Are we almost to the end?" Eddie asked. He was getting a bit restless. They had been walking by the water for more than an hour.

"Honestly, lad, I don't know how much farther it is. Frankly, I haven't made this trip before. Nor do I wish to make it again. This is one area of Dreamland that I do me best to avoid. Poisoned River offers nothin' but trouble. The Valley of Giants offers only the same. And just beyond that is the worst of all places."

"What's that?" Eddie asked.

"The Deserted Desert," said Sandy.

"What's so bad about that?"

"Well, you see, lad, right in the middle of it is the Canyon of Death."

Eddie gasped. Just the name sounded bad enough for him. "That's horrible."

"Aye, but not nearly as horrible as what's at the center of the Canyon of Death."

"What's there?"

"Dark Castle. Mortimer dried up a great lake and created the hottest, driest spot anywhere. He calls this waterless wasteland home. There's nothin' for miles around Dark Castle. He, and he alone, loves it there."

All this talk about the darker sides of Dreamland made Eddie pine for home even more. Dreamland did offer him adventure, but it offered more adventure than he had bargained for.

The pair continued along the river's bank. Eddie looked all around him. Mostly he looked out for rocks in the river. But he did notice that they were passing a lot of pine trees and that these were getting bigger and bigger as they went farther down the river. He mentioned this to Sandy.

"Aye, you're right," said Sandy. "Judgin' from the size of these trees, I should think we've reached the Valley of Giants. I hear their valley has the tallest trees anywhere, and these trees are definitely the tallest I've ever seen."

"I've seen taller," Eddie said matter-of-factly.

"Where?" asked Sandy.

"Why, back home—in California," said Eddie. "One year on vacation my parents took me to see the giant redwood trees. They're taller than these."

After another hour of walking, they were hungry. So they agreed to stop for lunch, thinking it best to walk a little ways from the river. That way they didn't have to be on the lookout for Water Bugs while they ate. Sandy picked a little clearing a hundred yards or so from the river. Because of the tall pines, the area was completely shaded. A tree stump in the middle of the clearing provided the perfect spot for lunch.

When they finished eating, Eddie took a good look around him. "Wow! Now these trees are the biggest, tallest I've ever seen."

"Then I'm sure we're in the Valley of Giants," said Sandy. "Now, not only must we watch out for Water Bugs, we must watch out for Giants as well. In fact, I think it would be safer for us to head back toward the river. And quietly, too."

Sandy didn't want to walk out in the open for fear a Giant would see them. So they made their way from tree to tree toward the river, walking quietly (if indeed it is possible to walk over thousands upon thousands of pine needles quietly). Both of them kept looking over their shoulders for Giants.

This constant looking back made them forget to look ahead. They forgot about the potential danger the river held. Before they realized it, they had reached Poisoned River. As Eddie watched the rapids race over some rocks, one of the rocks suddenly moved.

"Did you see that?"

"Did I see what?" Sandy asked in reply.

"That rock," said Eddie, pointing. "It moved."

Suddenly more "rocks" began moving toward Eddie and Sandy. There were perhaps two dozen of them.

"Uh-oh," said Sandy, "those aren't rocks. That's a whole herd of Water Bugs! Run or we're done for."

But they were already too close to escape. The Water Bugs nearest the shore had reached it. They were much bigger than cockroaches and much uglier, too. In front, they had two sharp pincers. Underneath, they had a couple dozen legs—and strong ones at that. Eddie watched them use these legs to propel themselves into the air. As they did so they rolled themselves into a ball, hurling airborne end over end toward the two travelers. Then they would uncurl themselves and land on their legs.

Unfortunately for Eddie and Sandy, the nearest Water Bugs were less than thirty feet away. So even as they attempted to run, the Water Bugs propelled themselves at the two faster than they could escape.

The pair stopped still and slowly backed away from the river toward the tall pines. One Water Bug hopped, rolled into a ball and sped in Sandy's direction. It uncurled and landed smack on a pine tree three feet in front of Sandy.

All Eddie could think of was how poisonous the Water Bugs were. He dearly wished to avoid them. The bugs had other intentions, altogether. One of them headed Eddie's way in its ball shape and landed smack on his jacket. He let out a loud scream and, using his arm, brushed the Water Bug off. They were dreadful creatures, and with so many of them Eddie could see no escape.

Just as he was thinking these dismal thoughts, another Water Bug hurled itself straight at his face. Well, the last place Eddie wanted a bug—any bug, let alone a Water Bug—was on his face, so he ducked. As he did so, he felt a whoosh of air above his head and heard a loud crack. Looking up, he saw the Water Bug flying quickly in the opposite direction. It flew much farther than it could hurl itself; in fact, it flew skyward until Eddie could see it no more.

While Eddie was watching this strange sight he heard another crack and turned to see where it was coming from. Behind him, club in hand, stood a Giant.

Eddie was really frightened now. He wasn't sure who to be more afraid of: the Water Bugs or the Giant. One look at what the Giant did with his club temporarily eased Eddie's fright and brought on awe. For the Giant wielded his club as a ballplayer would a bat. And with a perfect swing at the ball-shaped bugs, the Giant sent them flying farther than Eddie had ever seen anyone hit a baseball. Eddie wasn't certain whether the Giant was intending to help or whether he merely enjoyed this strange type of batting practice. But whatever his intentions, the Giant was helping. And for now, Eddie felt the safest place to be was behind this Giant.

Sandy tried to wave Eddie away from the Giant; however, as soon as a Water Bug flew at Sandy and was struck away by the Giant, he joined Eddie behind the big guy. As a Water Bug hurled itself toward Sandy and Eddie, the Giant hit it. Eddie and Sandy stayed huddled behind him as he continued to take his cuts at the bugs. Eddie was amazed. The Giant never once missed, and each hit was solid.

One of the bugs he hit zipped like a line drive and crashed into a tree on the other side of the river. Eddie was shocked to see this Water Bug uncurl itself and crawl away: The Giant's mighty blow seemed to have no effect on the Water Bug. As Sandy had told him, the bugs were indeed durable.

The last Water Bug soared straight at the Giant, who hit it solidly. He connected, sending the bug skyward, out of sight.

"Wow!" Eddie said in amazement.

Sandy, though, was tugging at Eddie's jacket. "Come on, lad, let's go or we'll have a bigger problem. That's a Giant."

"I see that," Eddie whispered back, "but he did save our lives."

"Perhaps. Perhaps he was only havin' fun. Look what he did to those bugs. Well, just look at *him*. Let's go."

Eddie took his first good look at the Giant. The Giant stood about ten feet tall. Muscles covered his body: His bulging biceps pushed against his white top; his legs, as big as tree stumps, tightly stretched his red britches. As Eddie was looking at the Giant, the Giant turned to the boy. His sharp eyes were as black as his skin and burned like coal into Eddie's eyes. The unsmiling Giant just stared at Eddie and let out a deep grunt.

The Giant's whole demeanor frightened Eddie. Not wanting to be ungrateful, though, Eddie let out a meek "Thank you." Then he and Sandy turned and ran.

They ran without looking back, and they ran until they could run no more. When they stopped, they turned around to look behind them. The coast was clear.

"We lost him," puffed Sandy, completely out of breath.

As the words left his mouth, they heard a deep, mocking laugh. Eddie and Sandy turned back toward the direction they had been running. Standing right in front of them with his arms crossed and his club at his side was the Giant.

"My name is Marques," the Giant said in a deep, booming voice, "and you cannot escape from me." Again, he gave his mocking laugh.

11

MARQUES THE GIANT

"What do you want with us?" Eddie asked Marques the Giant.

Marques seemed to ponder this question earnestly. His brow crinkled up, he put his fist to his chin and he tapped his cheek with his index finger.

"I haven't decided yet," he said at last.

"Come on, Eddie," Sandy whispered while tugging his charge away from the Giant, "we've at least got to try to escape."

"You're not going anywhere till I say you may," said the Giant.

Eddie stopped in his tracks, but Sandy still attempted to pull him away.

"We've got to go," urged Sandy in a hushed voice.

"I don't think he means us any harm, Sandy," Eddie said. "After all, if he did he could have smashed us to bits already."

"Lad, you don't understand the temperament of a Giant," Sandy said, exasperated. In his exasperation, he no longer whispered; instead, he raised his voice. "Any Giant means to cause harm—even a runt of a Giant like this one."

Marques, "the runt of a Giant" referred to, clearly took insult from this statement and growled as he raised his club over Sandy's head.

"How can you call him a runt of a Giant? Why, he's the biggest Giant I've ever seen," Eddie said sincerely.

Eddie's sincerity caught the Giant off guard; he lowered his club.

"I called him a runt, lad, because every other Giant I've ever seen would tower over this little one by a good five or six feet."

Again the Giant was angered and raised his club over Sandy.

"Nonsense," said Eddie. "Where I come from Giants are much shorter than this one. In fact, Marques would tower over them all."

Again the Giant lowered his club, but he had a puzzled look on his face. He raised his hand to his chin and tapped his cheek, thinking.

"Besides," Eddie said, "he did help us escape from the Water Bugs."

"He was only playin'," Sandy said. "He could do the same thing to us that he did to the Water Bugs—even if he is a giant runt."

"Hush," said Marques harshly as he brushed Sandy aside; not knowing his own strength, he pushed Sandy into the ground, where the little Sandman rolled three or four times before stopping. The Giant enjoyed that spectacle and laughed deeply. "I wouldn't be calling a Giant, any Giant, a runt if I were as puny as you are, little man." Then Marques spoke directly to Eddie: "I want to know if you are telling me the truth or pulling my leg."

"About what?" asked a slightly frightened Eddie.

"About Giants, of course. Giants from where you come from. Are they really shorter than me?"

"Oh, yes. You're a lot taller than them. Here, let me show you."

Eddie reached into his jacket pocket and pulled out his San Francisco Giant baseball cards. He handed them to Marques.

Marques went through them, but seemed unimpressed. "I can't tell how tall they are from these pictures."

"Oh, but you can," said Eddie. He turned one over and pointed, "Their heights are listed on the back."

"Six-foot-four!" The Giant slapped his thigh and roared with laughter. "Six-foot-four is tiny."

"Look at this one," Eddie said, pulling out Joe Ortiz. "He's my favorite."

"Five-foot-nine? There must be some kind of mistake," the Giant said, frowning.

"No mistake, he's the shortest Giant. But he is a Giant," Eddie said.

"So I see. He has a club in hand and all. A five-foot-nine Giant, imagine that. I'd be tall, gloriously tall. Where do I find these puny Giants?"

"In the Real World," said Sandy.

"I should have known," said Marques. "Here in Dreamland, I am a little Giant and the normal Giants want little to do with me. If only there were a way that I could show them one of these smaller Giants, but, alas, they are from the Real World."

"You can show them Joe Ortiz's card," Eddie said.

"But you said this card is your favorite," Marques said.

"It is my favorite, but you can keep it. After all, you did save our lives."

Marques sat down on a rock, put the card in his shirt pocket and began to sob softly. "Why are you being so nice to me? No one's ever been nice to me."

"I happen to like Giants," Eddie said.

"Let's go now, lad," whispered Sandy, recognizing a good opportunity when he saw one.

Marques sat, fist to chin, finger to cheek, pondering. He had stopped his initial emotional outburst. Suddenly, he stood up and snapped his fingers. "I've got it," he declared. "If there is anything I can do for you—anything *nice*, I mean—let me know."

"But you already did: You saved our lives," Eddie said.

"Oh, that, no, no, no," Marques said while waving his hand. "That doesn't count, that was by accident." In a penitent tone, he added, "You see, I *was* just having fun. I want to do something nice."

"Well, maybe you *can* help us," Eddie said.

"Oh, no," Sandy said, waving both hands in front of him and shaking his head vigorously.

"How?" asked Marques excitedly.

"Eddie, I really don't think this is such a good idea," said Sandy.

"I think a Giant may be just what we need," said Eddie. "Besides, he offered his help and I'm sure he means it."

"Oh, I do, I do," said Marques.

"Well," thought Sandy out loud, "okay, but don't say I didn't warn you, lad."

Eddie took the cue and began recounting his experiences in Dreamland for Marques. He told him everything, concluding about ten minutes later with: ". . . So for me to go back home, we must find Beni at the river's end. Do you think you can help us? If you can't—or don't want to—it's all right."

"That's a sad story," Marques said. "I've had a brush with Mortimer myself. He's a real nasty fellow. I'd really rather avoid him completely. But I can help you, so I will. I'll get you to the river's end ten times faster than you would have gotten there. Plus, I'll protect you from Water Bugs along the way."

"Deal," said Sandy loudly. Sandy's comment caught all three—including Sandy—by surprise. Both Eddie and Marques laughed while Sandy smiled and shrugged his shoulders.

Marques quickly got down to business. He pulled an axe from his tool belt and chopped down a giant tree in no time flat. He then split the trunk in half, cut it down a little and began shaping it. Before too long he had a canoe. He lifted it over his head and carried it to the river. Setting it by the river, he returned to make two oars from some of the scrap wood. He tossed them into the canoe and pushed the narrow boat into the water.

"Let's go," said the Giant.

133

Eddie and Sandy hopped into the boat. Marques gave a huge shove off the shore and jumped in with them. He steered the canoe to the center of the river and pointed it down the currents.

"It sure beats walking, doesn't it?" asked Marques the Giant. Eddie and Sandy agreed readily, for the canoe moved at a good clip.

Eddie was amazed by the view offered from the river. They were now in the heart of the Valley of Giants—and what a spectacular valley it was. Beautiful trees, tall rocks and distant mountains made for an awe-inspiring view. Only one word could have accurately captured Eddie's feelings: "Wow!" And he said that word many times as the canoe rushed down the river.

The river twisted and turned a number of times. Eddie could not always see far ahead because of these turns. After the canoe rounded one such bend, a dozen or so Water Bugs attacked them. Marques dispensed with them quickly, giving each a crushing blow that sent it far out of sight. Eddie marveled at Marques's skill in using his club.

"Where I come from, your hitting would be in great demand," said Eddie after Marques had taken care of all the Bugs. Eddie was thinking how his Giants—the baseball ones— could use such an impressive hitter.

Marques, looking truly flattered by the comment, thanked Eddie.

"You know," Sandy said after they had gone farther down the river, "it probably would've taken us till nightfall to get this far walkin'."

"We'll get all the way to Beni long before nightfall," Marques said. "In fact, we'll make it to the river's end within the hour."

"Do you know where the river ends?" asked Eddie.

"Certainly," Marques said, "it ends at the third waterfall."

"At the *third* waterfall?" Sandy asked. "Why, we haven't even seen one waterfall."

"Oh, they come one after the other," said the Giant.

"And just how do you propose to maneuver this canoe over three waterfalls?" asked Sandy.

"To be honest, I hadn't thought about it," Marques said, putting his fist to his chin and tapping his cheek with his index finger. The canoe made its way around another of the river's many bends.

"You'd better start thinkin' about it!" yelled Sandy. "Look!"

Up ahead of the canoe the river seemed to disappear in a mad gush: the first waterfall! A huge oak tree stood on the right side of the river near the waterfall. Its giant branches stretched a third of the way across the waterfall, a good fifteen feet above the river. On the other side of the river, there was nothing but rocks.

"I didn't realize we had come so far already," said Marques calmly.

"Well, we have. Now what are you goin' to do?" said Sandy. Then he turned to Eddie and said, "I toldcha takin' a Giant was a big mistake."

Marques did not seem at all concerned. He continued to paddle toward the waterfall, but bearing to the right.

"Are you crazy?" shouted Sandy. "You should steer us away from the fall."

"Can't. The current's too strong," Marques said. "Fight Mother Nature and Mother Nature wins every time. I prefer to go with the flow."

Marques brought the canoe as close to the right bank as he could in the time he had, but they still remained ten feet from shore as the canoe reached the waterfall. Marques made a last-second correction, straightening the canoe out directly under the outstretched branches of the oak tree.

Undaunted, Marques stood up and said, "Grab onto me and hold on tight."

Both Eddie and Sandy obeyed without question. Marques grabbed his club with his left hand and raised his right arm up to its full length. He reached for the outstretched branch of the oak tree hanging over the waterfall. The front of the canoe came to the edge of the fall and started over it. When it was about half way over the waterfall, the nose bent down and began to fall. Just at that instant, Marques grabbed hold of the branch. Eddie watched the empty canoe crash against the rocks at the bottom of the hundred-foot fall, breaking into several pieces.

"Would you mind holding my club?" Marques asked.

"What?" said Sandy, shocked. "You want us to let go of you to hold yer club when we're hangin' on for dear life? No way."

"Never mind then," said the Giant.

Indeed, Sandy did have a valid point. The three of them were hanging well over the waterfall, supported by one creaking branch. To make matters worse, Marques held the branch with only one arm, while Sandy and Eddie clung to him, and not to the branch. So the entire weight of all three was supported by the strength of one arm—and one branch. Meanwhile, that branch began to bend from all the weight. Marques, still unconcerned, merely tossed his club behind his back, placing it right at the foot of the huge oak tree. He then spit on his left hand and placed it on the branch next to his right hand. Bringing his right hand down, he spit on it and returned it to the branch. The creaking of the branch continued, and Eddie, eyeing the branch, saw it splitting near the trunk.

"I hate to tell you this," Eddie said, "but the branch is breaking."

"I don't doubt that for a minute," grunted Marques as he swung his body parallel to the bank. "After all, we do have a lot of weight on it."

Marques placed his left hand over his right; then he brought his right hand over his left. Hand over hand, he brought them toward the bank while the branch cracked and sank. When they were only a few feet from the river's bank, the branch gave way, breaking downward. It broke at an angle toward the tree's trunk; as it came down, Eddie, Sandy and Marques landed just onto the bank.

"That was a lucky break," Marques said as he picked up his club. With a grin, he added, "Well, what are you guys waiting for? Let's go."

Both Eddie and Sandy looked dazed. Unlike Marques, they had not landed on their feet.

"I don't know if I can take any more of this excitement," Sandy said.

"That was way too scary," Eddie said, picking himself up off the ground.

"Look," said Marques. He was standing at the edge of the bank near the waterfall. Eddie and Sandy joined him to see what he was pointing at. "I noticed this while we were clinging to the branch. You can see both of the other falls from here. There's the second and there is the third. See?"

The waterfalls did not seem to be that far away—only about a hundred feet straight down and less than three football fields to the next fall. Then not quite that far to the third.

"There, at the third waterfall, we will find Beni," said Marques.

"And I will get home!" shouted Eddie.

"Well, what are we waitin' for?" said Sandy. "Let's get a move on."

12

BENI

Eddie and Sandy followed Marques's giant steps down the rocky cliff to the foot of the first waterfall. There the ground leveled out. When they reached the second waterfall, the mountain headed sharply down again.

From the top of that waterfall, Eddie could see where the third fall dropped off. Beyond it, the land became more and more barren, and Eddie could not make out where the river went from there. It seemed to completely disappear.

Puzzled, he asked, "Where does the river go after the third waterfall."

"It ends," Sandy and Marques said together.

Sandy continued solo, " 'Tis at the end of the river where we're to find Beni, right, lad?"

"Right," said Eddie, but he was still puzzled as to where the river went.

The trio climbed down this second drop and again it leveled with the river. The third waterfall rushed over the edge a short distance away. One thought and one thought alone excited Eddie: returning home! Eddie long ago had decided that the adventures of Dreamland were too intense and too dangerous for one from the Real World. He desperately wished to return to his world. He longed for the joys of playing outdoors with his friends; of visiting beautiful spots in his world; of going to more ball games with his father; yes, even of finishing his project. Now Eddie's goal was in sight. All he had to do was reach the wizard, Beni, who would cast a spell more powerful than Mortimer's, removing his curse from the sand. Then Eddie would be home.

With this happy thought, Eddie ran to the third waterfall. When he reached it, he looked over the edge and watched the water tumble down. At the bottom of the fall, he saw something he had never seen before: The water hit the rocks below, some of it even splashed back up, but the river ended right there. The whole river spilled over the fall, down onto the rocks and then vanished entirely.

"Where's the river?" asked a bewildered Eddie.

"It ends, it ends" said his two companions, slightly out of sync. True enough, the river ended.

"But it can't just end," Eddie said. "The water has to go some place."

"See for yerself, lad," Sandy said. "It just ends. I see nothin' so very strange about that."

Unlike Sandy, Eddie saw nothing at all usual about it.

"This waterfall is the steepest," said Marques. "We can't climb down here. We'll have to wind our way down over there and circle back to it."

Eddie and Sandy followed Marques down the rocky path to the foot of the mountain. Then they doubled back toward the waterfall.

As they did, Eddie looked around and was amazed at the contrasts on either side of him. To his left, the mountain they had just descended stood covered with its various kinds of trees. It was lush and beautiful: green where the trees stood, gray where the rock was. To his right, however, an entirely different view presented itself. The land became more and more parched. Besides cactus, the arid land had little vegetation of any kind. The wind kicked up sand in places. The unbelievable contrast made Eddie feel he was walking between two incompatible, misplaced landscapes.

Soon the waterfall came into view. Eddie forgot about the contrasts and remembered home. He ran toward the fall. Sandy and Marques followed. Marques, with his huge strides, easily outdistanced the other two and arrived first. Eddie made it second, well ahead of Sandy, who reached it completely out of breath.

Eddie peered all around the waterfall and again he was puzzled. The river did not run down to the left or to the right. Nor did it run underground. The water inexplicably disappeared. Since neither of his two friends seemed to think it odd that the river stopped, Eddie did not bother to ask any more questions about it.

Instead, he asked a more important question. "Where do you suppose Beni is?"

"I suppose Beni is right here," Marques said. "Somewhere."

" 'Tis the end of the river," said Sandy, frowning, "but I don't see where Beni can be."

The threesome paced in front of the waterfall for some time. Sandy scratched his head and shook it. Marques put his fist on his chin and with his index finger tapped his cheek. Eddie was too confused to know what to think.

"I've got it!" Marques declared, snapping his fingers. "Beni is right here, right now. Watching us."

"That's ridiculous," said Sandy. "Why would Beni just watch us?"

"To find out if we can be trusted. We must tell Beni why we're here."

"That will never work," said Sandy.

"Maybe not," Eddie said, "but it's worth a try." Eddie turned and faced the waterfall. Loudly he said, "My name is Eddie. This is Sandy and that's Marques. We have traveled here to get your help. Beni, if you're here, please help me get back home, back to the Real World."

Eddie stopped talking and all three waited in hushed anticipation, but nothing happened.

"I toldcha it wouldn't work," said Sandy.

No sooner were the words out of his mouth than a flame appeared on the other side of the waterfall. The trio watched as the fire moved through the water without being extinguished. It stopped right in front of the visitors.

A loud voice, deep but distorted, said, "You who seek the wizard, Beni, follow the flame."

The fire moved back through and behind the waterfall. Eddie, Sandy and Marques looked at each other hesitantly. Then they all shrugged their shoulders and followed the fire. They walked through the waterfall and came out completely dry.

"Wow!" said Eddie. "We didn't get wet."

The flame continued to move down a corridor in front of them, lighting up a cavern as it did so.

"Of course!" said Eddie. "Beni lives in a hidden cave behind the waterfall." Eddie felt Beni's protection against Mortimer was more clever than building a castle out of sand or out of ice.

They followed the flame down this narrow tunnel. It turned to the right and opened into a huge room. Entering it, the flame vanished.

In this room stood a little girl dressed in a frilly blue dress.

"You seek the wizard, Beni?" asked the little girl.

"Yes," said Eddie. "Where is he?"

The little girl smiled and asked, "What do you want Beni to do for you?"

"I want Beni to send me back home," Eddie said. "Do you know where we can find him?"

"Yes," said the little girl, "but first you must hand over the magic wand."

"What?" asked Eddie.

"The magic wand," said the little girl, "hand it over."

"I just want to know where Beni is and whether he can help me or not," said Eddie.

"Of course Beni can help you," said the little girl, "once you hand over the wand."

"We don't have a magic wand," said Eddie.

"You must," said the little girl, raising her voice.

"Great. You mean we have to go on some wild goose chase looking for a magic wand?" Eddie was getting a little upset himself. "I don't even know what this wand looks like. Why can't Beni just help us. After all, he's supposed to be a great wizard."

"Beni is a great wizard," said the girl sharply, "but you had best stop calling Beni by the masculine gender."

"What?" Eddie didn't quite understand.

"Didn't anyone tell you?" asked Marques.

"Tell me what?" said Eddie.

"Why, that the great wizard, Beni, is female," said Marques.

"What?" said Eddie.

"What did you expect?" asked the little girl.

"Well, I expected a wizard to be, well, you know, an old man with white hair and a beard."

"Oh, a stereotypical wizard," said the little girl as she crossed her arms.

"Besides," said Eddie, "what kind of name is Beni for a woman."

"What kind of name is Eddie for a man?" asked the little girl.

"Why, it's just fine," said Eddie.

"And so is mine," said the little girl. "After all, Beni is the name my mother gave me."

Eddie stood silently, blinking and thinking, for a full minute before he said, "You can't be Beni—I mean not Beni the wizard."

"I am, indeed," said the little girl.

"Oh, great," said Eddie, dismayed. "We travel half way around Dreamland looking for a powerful wizard who can send me home and all we find is a girl. I may never get home!"

"You have to change your attitude," said Beni, "or you'll get no help from me at all."

"You won't help us," Eddie said angrily, "unless we give you a magic wand anyway."

"So you admit it," said Beni, also angrily.

"Admit what?" said Eddie. Sandy and Marques stood behind Eddie. Both looked as though they felt the conversation was going badly.

"Admit to knowing what I'm talking about," said Beni.

"I really don't think any of us knows what you're talkin' about, lass," said Sandy,

147

attempting to calm down both Eddie and Beni. But they were both too upset by now.

"She can't help me," said Eddie. "She's just a girl."

"And you're just a boy, trapped in my world," said Beni. "See if you get my help."

She brushed past the three of them with a huff and headed down the tunnel toward the waterfall. Sandy and Marques both looked shocked. They each grabbed Eddie and followed after Beni.

"You can't let her go like that, lad," said Sandy. "She's yer last hope."

"Then I have no hope," said Eddie. "Let her go. She's no wizard anyway."

"I am too a wizard," shouted Beni, as she turned back toward them. "Watch this."

A flame appeared in each of her hands and she hurled them above the heads of her audience.

"Wow!" said an amazed Eddie.

"Humph," said Beni as she turned on her heels, tossed back her head and exited through the waterfall.

"Wow! I guess she really is a wizard."

"Of course she really is a wizard," said Sandy, "but I doubt seriously that she will help you now."

"Why didn't you tell me that Beni was a little girl?" asked Eddie.

"Because I didn't think it important, lad. I thought it was important to know that Beni was a wizard. What difference did it make whether the wizard was young or old, male or female. After all, you yerself said that a wizard was exactly what we needed."

Marques, who had been tapping his cheek, said, "I think the best thing for you to do is to apologize to her, Eddie."

"No way," said Eddie. "We'll have to find another way out of Dreamland."

"Lad, I never thought I'd be sayin' this, but I agree with the Giant. You should apologize."

"But Beni wasn't at all what I expected," said Eddie.

"So?" said Marques. "We don't always get what we expect. Sometimes what we get turns out to be even better than what we expected."

"I don't think so, Marques," said Eddie. "Beni got awfully mad at me for no reason at all."

"And you got awfully mad back," said the Giant. "I saw no good reason for your anger."

"Nor did I, lad," Sandy said, "I think for all concerned, you should tell her you're sorry."

"All right," said Eddie.

"Good," said Sandy. "Now let's go after her."

The three walked down the tunnel and through the waterfall. When they came out the other side they were soaking wet.

"Why, that little wizard," said Marques. But all three laughed.

13

THE DECEPTION

Marques and Sandy shared a good laugh over Beni's joke, but Eddie remained shaken. Beni was nowhere to be seen.

"Where do you suppose she went?" asked Eddie. "Oh, it's all my fault. But how was I supposed to know she was a wizard? Boy, could she hurl that fire though."

"I don't know where she went," said the Giant, shaking his head. "It's too bad you made her mad—she really is the best good wizard in Dreamland."

"I wonder when she'll be back," said Sandy. "Or if she'll be back."

Eddie cupped his hands around his mouth and yelled, "Beni! Beni!"

He stood still, but the only answer he received was his own voice echoing back "Beni!"

Forlorn, he moaned, "Oh, I really hope she'll help me."

Suddenly, from the far side of the mountain, they saw Beni making her way back. She was skipping merrily along as if nothing at all had happened. In her hand she held a wand.

Marques, noticing the wand, said, "She must have gone to fetch the magic wand herself. I think she may help you after all."

By now, Beni was about twenty steps away. Eddie called to her, "You're back!"

"Of course I'm back," said Beni. "You need my help, don't you?"

"Oh, yes, yes, I do," said Eddie. "Oh, and I'm sorry."

"Sorry for what?" asked Beni.

"Why, sorry for calling you a girl," said Eddie.

"But I am a girl," said the little wizard.

"Boy, when she has a change of heart, she really has a change of heart," said Marques, puzzled.

"You mean you're not mad at me?" asked Eddie.

"Not now," said Beni.

"I mean, after all, I did say you weren't much of a wizard," said Eddie.

152

"Quit while you're ahead, lad," whispered Sandy.

"Oh, that. Calling me a girl and not much of a wizard. Let's let bygones be bygones, shall we?" Beni smiled.

"Sure," said Eddie. "Wow, a real wizard. What you did with the fire was something else."

"You haven't seen anything yet," said Beni. "But really, if you expect me to help you we must begin right away. Follow me."

Eddie, Sandy and Marques obediently began to follow her when a voice from behind called out, "Just where do you guys think you're going?"

The three of them turned around and, much to their surprise, found themselves looking right at Beni. Eddie turned his head back the other way and saw Beni there as well. Both were dressed identically. The only difference was that the one they were following held a wand, the other had none.

"They're twins!" said the Giant.

"We are *not* twins," said the little girl without the wand.

"We most *definitely* are not," said the girl holding the wand.

Sandy, Marques and Eddie all turned their heads back and forth as though they were watching a tennis match while each "Beni" spoke.

The girls threw this rhythm off, though, as each simultaneously pointed a finger at the other and said: "He's Mortimer."

"I don't see one 'he' between you," said Marques.

"You silly Giant," said the girl with the wand, "don't you see that Mortimer is pulling the Deception on you."

"The Deception?" asked Marques, looking very puzzled.

"Yes, the Deception," said the other girl. "It's an ancient trick, a rather simple one requiring only that the wizard performing it be holding a magic wand."

Eddie, Marques and Sandy instinctively moved toward the girl who wasn't holding a wand.

"It's an ancient trick, all right," said the girl with the wand, "but you don't need a wand to perform it. Do you guys really believe that Mortimer would need a wand to perform a simple trick?"

Eddie, Marques and Sandy immediately moved back toward the girl with the wand.

"But you do need to be holding a wand!" said the girl without it.

"Do not!"

"Do too!"

"Do not!"

"Girls!" yelled Sandy above the bantering. "There must be some way to figure out which of you is really you and which is Mortimer. You both agree that one of you is Beni and one is Mortimer, right?"

Both girls nodded and said, "Right."

Then the one with the wand said, "Eddie, we're wasting time. This is exactly what Mortimer would want to happen. Unless we hurry, Mortimer will steal your imagination in no time."

"Steal his imagination?" said the wizard without the wand to the other one. "So that's what you've been up to."

Eddie, Sandy and Marques again moved away from the wizard with the wand.

"He's just trying another ploy to trick you," said the wizard holding the wand. "Pretending he doesn't know about wanting your imagination. I'm a wizard and don't need to be told such things—I know. Even before you came down the river by canoe, I knew you were coming to see me. Long before you made me mad."

The three again moved toward the girl with the wand.

"Wait a minute," said the wandless wizard. "How does he know I was mad at you?"

"I know because I was there," said the wizard with the wand.

"Oh no, you weren't."

"Yes, I was. He called me a girl."

"The boy also said I wasn't much of a wizard," said the wizard without the wand.

"How did she know that?" asked Eddie, addressing the wizard with the wand, but pointing at the one without it.

"Maybe she overheard you apologizing to me," said the girl with the wand.

"You apologized to me?" asked the other. Eddie nodded.

"I *shall* help you then," said the girl without the wand. "After all, I was mad because I thought you had stolen my wand. I didn't realize Mortimer had."

"I'm Beni, and I have no reason to steal my own wand," said the girl with the wand. "As you can see, I'm holding it. I went to get it to help you."

"I'll settle this once and for all," said the girl without the wand. "I can prove I am who I am. Watch me!"

She ran toward the waterfall and stopped in front of it.

"It's a trick," said the girl holding the wand.

"The only trick here is the Deception," said the girl by the waterfall. "Holding that wand, a wizard can take on any physical resemblance he or she desires. But the Deception does not deceive the deceiver. Mortimer, though he may look exactly like me,

156

is not me. He is still Mortimer. And he, unlike me, is still vulnerable to water."

With this the girl turned and ran through the waterfall. She then ran back out, completely dry. Looking at the other wizard, she dared, "Now, Mortimer, you try that."

Something terrible began to happen to the little girl holding the wand. She began to grow and change. When her appearance stopped changing, Mortimer, with his ugly ashen features, stood before them.

"You win, for now, Beni," he said in his evil voice. "But without your wand—this wand that I hold—you are powerless to stop me."

Turning to Marques, Mortimer said, "You, you stupid Giant. Once was not enough for you, was it? Well, we shall see about that. I promise you here and now that if you continue to help this boy, I'll do worse than simply cutting you down to half your size."

Marques backed up two steps in horror, saying, "No, no."

Turning sharply to Eddie, Mortimer said, "And you, boy, your time is almost up. I wanted to do this the easy way and take you with me by your own choice. I cannot force you to come—yet. I have time, so I shall wait. You don't have time, so you shall come to me. You will come to me, for I hold the power!" Mortimer raised the wand above his head, laughing wickedly. "I, and I alone, control Dreamland. Never forget that. Yes, you will come to me to die. And through your death, I will gain an imagination."

Mortimer threw back his vulturelike head and again laughed a deep, evil laugh. Then, with a puff of smoke, he vanished.

Eddie was badly shaken. The first time he had seen Mortimer he was frightened, but this time was worse.

"We almost went with him, Sandy," said Eddie.

"The Deception is a powerful and effective spell," said Beni. "Anyone could fall for it, maybe even a little girl." Eddie smiled. "I'm sorry, too, Eddie. Sorry that I got mad at you. But you see, just before you got here, while I was out gathering berries, my wand was stolen. I thought it a little more than a coincidence that you three should show up shortly after my wand disappeared. So naturally I suspected you had something to do with it. Now I see I had it wrong, even though I had it right."

"Huh?" said Sandy.

Beni smiled. "I'm surprised you should question a paradox, Sandy, what with a Sandman's love for them. Indeed, you did have something to do with it, indirectly;

though, directly you had nothing to do with it. Anyway, I'm truly sorry I can't help you."

"But you can," said Eddie. "You have to."

"I would, if I could, but I can't. For, you see, without my wand I am not much of a wizard at all."

"But that's not true," said Eddie. "I saw what you did with the fire. That took a real wizard. And then we walked through the waterfall without getting wet. That took a real wizard, too."

"Child's play," muttered the wizard. "Basic, elementary wizardry. Why, with a little practice, anyone could master those tricks. I'm afraid that the Fire and Ice Spell is the only spell I can perform without my wand. I can do you little good."

Marques, who had been tapping his cheek, suddenly snapped his fingers and said, "I've got it! We must get your wand back."

"That would be playin' right into Mortimer's hands," said Sandy. "It's exactly what he expects us to do."

"Still," said Beni, "it is the only thing we have left to do that gives us any hope at all."

"We'll have to do it without Eddie, then," said Sandy. "Otherwise, he won't be safe once Dark Castle is in sight."

"Yes," said Beni, "that is best."

"But there's not enough time," said Marques. "We can't get there and back before Eddie's time runs out. Like it or not, Eddie must come with us."

"You're right, Marques," said Sandy. "I'd forgotten how little time we have left."

"It's nice that you're all willing to help me, but I can't ask you to go up against Mortimer. Besides, Marques, I heard what Mortimer said to you. He warned you not to help me."

"But that won't stop me," said Marques.

"You've done enough already," said Eddie. "What happened between you and Mortimer anyway?"

"Well, it's a long story," Marques said. "And I think long stories are best left untold when time is short."

"I know the story well," said Beni. "The long and short of it is that Marques is too modest to tell it himself. Once, he was the strongest and tallest of all Giants, standing nearly twenty feet. Mortimer created an evil, fire-breathing dragon and trained the dragon to kill Giants. You see, Mortimer wanted to wipe out all Giants in Dreamland. Marques, in an effort to save his race, killed the dragon and made Mortimer mad."

"He cast a spell upon me," said Marques, "that he said would prove to be a fate worse

than death: He made me half my size. His
prediction proved correct. As Mighty Marques,
I was loved by my people; as a little runt, I was
ridiculed and abandoned. Why, even that little
Sandman called me a runt. No one wanted
anything to do with a runt of a Giant—until
you came, Eddie. And I will help you."

"You were Mighty Marques?" said an
awed Sandy. "Why, I've heard many a tale
aboutcha. You were the strongest of all the
Giants."

"And I still am," said Marques. "Though
Mortimer thinks he left me with only half my
size and strength, his spell robbed me only of
my size. I still have all of my strength. I can
still beat any Giant."

"And to think I nearly made you mad
enough to do me in," said a shocked Sandy.
"Why, sir, 'tis an honor to have yer help."

The Giant and the tiny Sandman shook
hands, with Sandy's hand fitting between
Marques's thumb and index finger.

"I really can't let you guys help me any
more," said Eddie. "I think it might be best to
just let Mortimer have my imagination."

"Oh, no," said Beni. "When Mortimer
tipped his hand by admitting he was after
your imagination, I knew things were serious.
Mortimer, with an imagination from the Real
World, would be infinitely more dangerous

than he is already. I think we must do what Marques suggests. We must go after the wand. It is not only your last hope, Eddie—it is ours as well. All of Dreamland depends upon our success. I, too, will do what I can to help. We can get to the edge of the Canyon of Death by nightfall, if we hurry."

"But we must leave now, even though it's a bad time to go," said Sandy.

"It is, however, the only time Mortimer wouldn't expect us," said Marques. "I mean, who would be foolish enough to head down into the Canyon of Death when it is being patrolled by Trogs?"

"Trogs!" exclaimed Eddie in horror. "I thought we had seen the last of them."

"Everywhere there are caves, there are Trogs," said Marques. "If we are to sneak up on Mortimer successfully, I'm afraid you'll have to face Trogs once more."

"I'm afraid he's right," said Sandy.

Eddie was just afraid.

14

TROGS!

The four schemers went back inside Beni's cave to ready themselves for their journey. Marques pulled a canvas backpack from his tool belt, unfolded it, and loaded supplies into it.

"Don't forget this," said Beni. In her arms she cradled a huge book, the *Book of Spells*, just like the one ancient Sherman used in Sandsibar.

"Wow," said Eddie. "A spell book. Does everyone in Dreamland have one?"

"Not everyone," said Beni as Marques packed the book, "but you can bet Mortimer does. He is the most learned of all when it comes to the *Book of Spells*. He has spent centuries studying it. I have barely begun to read it. I do know, though, that I need only to use the right Dispel Spell."

"The right what?" Eddie asked.

"Dispel Spell,"repeated Beni. "There are dozens of them—each with a varying degree of difficulty. All of them hold a wizard powerless for a short time. The most difficult of all would be the best one to use; however, for it to work, it requires a second wizard giving a rhyming line to end it. And how would I get Mortimer to do that? So I'll just have to use one that dispels the spell Mortimer cast. But I need my wand to cast it."

"Why?" asked Eddie. "Mortimer doesn't use one."

"True," said Beni, "but I'm still a wizard-in-training. Mortimer is a master at wizardry and can perform most spells without the need of any magical apparatus—of course, even he needs it for spells like the Deception which require it. Not yet true for me. To me, the magic wand is the most important thing."

"The most important thing for me is a long, strong rope," said Marques as he grabbed a thick fifty-foot rope, coiled it and placed it into his pack.

Marques slung the loaded pack on his back and headed toward the opening of the cave. The other three followed him. They emerged from the waterfall completely dry.

Eddie gazed toward the increasingly barren horizon ahead of them.

"We're at the outermost edge of the Deserted Desert," said Beni as her eyes followed Eddie's gaze. "Mortimer stopped the flow of the river so that he could have a waterless home. He even dried up a great lake to create the Canyon of Death. Then he built Dark Castle on what used to be an underwater ledge. This journey won't be easy, and it won't be fun."

"Aye, but we must make it," said Sandy.

"Yes," said Beni. "So let's go."

Following Beni's lead, Eddie, Sandy and Marques headed away from the waterfall toward the barren horizon. The farther they walked, the more bleak the picture looked ahead of them; behind them, the landscape grew progressively greener. Given the choice, the difference would make any traveler turn around; these four, unfortunately, were given no choice. And so, reluctantly, they pressed on. Soon they reached an area where not even cactus grew. On the horizon behind them, the cactus itself looked inviting; on the horizon ahead, they saw nothing—miles and miles of nothing. On into this nothingness the travelers ventured, until the view became equally bleak in all directions.

"We are getting close now," said Beni. "I recognize the telltale signs of nothing."

They walked on into the unchanging "signs of nothing" for a solid hour—but such a completely boring and exhausting hour that to Eddie it seemed like three.

"Aren't we there yet?" he asked when he could take no more. It seemed odd even to him that he should be anxious to arrive at a place he wished he didn't have to go to at all.

"Look," said Marques, "I can see the edge of the Canyon of Death."

Marques pointed directly in front of them. Eddie saw nothing but nothing.

"Where?" he asked.

"There." Marques pointed. Then, realizing something, he lifted Eddie upon his giant shoulders. "There. Can you see it?"

From this height, Eddie could see some change in color as the desert turned black at the horizon.

"The Canyon of Death," said Marques.

"We must get there fast," said Sandy, "so we can get down it before dark. I don't have to remind anyone of what happens at night."

With this renewed sense of purpose, the voyagers ran toward the Canyon of Death. They ran as quickly toward it as most sane people would run away from it.

The black hole on the horizon became bigger and bigger as they ran closer to it.

"Wow!" muttered Eddie, pulling to a stop at the canyon's rim. Eddie had never seen the Canyon of Death before, but he had seen the Grand Canyon while on vacation one summer. The Canyon of Death held little resemblance to the gorge in Arizona. This canyon was much deeper and darker. And far more menacing. With the sun hovering near the horizon behind them, the whole canyon was one dark shadow to which the eyes slowly adjusted.

"Here it is, the Canyon of Death," said Beni.

"Wow," said Eddie. "Why is it called the Canyon of Death?"

"Because," said Sandy, giving the answer Eddie feared, "no one who has entered it has ever returned alive."

"No one? Not even one person?" asked Eddie.

"No one," said Sandy, shaking his head. "Not even one person."

"Unless you count Mortimer," said Beni.

"We better hurry," said Marques. "We want to get as far down as we can before the Trogs come out."

Eddie felt Marques's enthusiasm was out of place, coming on the heels of Sandy's dire words. And the mention of Trogs didn't thrill him either.

"Isn't there any way we can avoid them?" asked Eddie.

"I hope so, but I doubt it," said Marques. "Just look at all those caves."

Eddie looked down. Everywhere he looked he saw ledges—disjointed, uneven and narrow. And at nearly every ledge he saw at least one cave. Small caves, large caves; caves which led to ledges and caves which didn't. The whole face of the canyon was as pitted with caves as the moon is with craters. Getting down this canyon would be difficult enough without Trogs. With Trogs, it might be impossible. It looked impossible already.

"How in the world are we going to get down?" asked Eddie.

"We'll have to climb down from ledge to ledge. Once we reach the bottom, we can walk to the foot of the rock where Dark Castle is. Then we'll have to climb up to it," said Marques.

"But the ledges aren't close enough," said Eddie, seeing that they really weren't. Nor did they seem to be arranged in any kind of accessible pattern.

"You leave that problem to me," said Marques.

"Where is Dark Castle anyway?" asked Eddie.

"You'll see it soon enough," said Sandy, "and once you do, lad, you'll no longer be safe."

Eddie remembered what Sherman had told him: Once in view of Dark Castle,

168

Mortimer could take him by force—if Mortimer were aware of his presence. Luckily, thought Eddie, they had secretly made this journey. "Mortimer doesn't know we're here, right?" he asked for reassurance.

"He has no idea whatsoever," said Sandy. "I hope."

"Yeah," said Eddie, "me, too. How long will it take us to get there?"

"All night, I should think," said the Giant. "Maybe a little longer."

"That only gives us a couple of hours to find the wand so I can break that spell and fix your sand," said Beni. "And only you, Sandy, can get him back asleep."

"Aye, once the sand is good again. But we're pushin' it awfully close. I only hope we can do it all before it's too late. And we're not goin' to do any of it if we don't get started." Sandy glanced at Marques, who stood with his fist to his chin. "Well, Marques, shouldn't we be startin'?" Sandy tentatively added.

"Oh, I'm sorry," said the Giant. "I was just figuring the best path down."

Marques walked about twenty yards to the left, where he pulled the rope out of his backpack. He lowered the rope down to the first ledge, which was about eighteen feet below them. Motioning for the others, he held the rope while they climbed down. Then

Marques dropped the rope to them, swung his body over the canyon and dropped himself down—a huge drop for Eddie, Beni or Sandy, but nothing at all for a ten-foot Giant with his arms extended fully above his head.

"Another couple hundred ledges and we'll be there," said Marques. His smile broke the tension and everyone smiled.

Marques looked down first one side of the ledge and then the other, tapping his cheek as he did so. He decided upon the next ledge, one about twelve feet below them and slightly to the right. He lowered the rope and held it while the others climbed down. Then he again swung his body over the precipice and pushed off it onto the one below. Down nearly twenty ledges the foursome went in this manner.

" 'Tis gettin' dark," said Sandy. This far down they were completely immersed in the dark shadows of the Canyon of Death. But more dangerously, day was quickly turning into night. And nighttime was no time for anyone to be venturing into Trog territory. Sounds of activity, within the walls of the canyon, echoed around the four travelers.

Eddie glanced nervously at the cave on the other end of the ledge they stood on. Noises could be heard from within it.

"Trogs," whispered Marques. "Everywhere. And this next ledge won't be easy to get to."

170

Marques surveyed both sides. There was not a landing place close to either side. Marques had carefully selected ledges four or five in advance to make the descent as easy as possible. A few ledges back he had realized that no matter which route he chose, this level presented no easy solutions. He now picked the ledge that looked closest. Still, it was about twelve feet away—and about twenty-five feet down. Marques stood tapping his cheek, deep in thought.

"I'll tell you what I'll have to do. I'll have to lower each of you one at a time and swing you over to that ledge. Once you are over it, you'll have to let go of the rope and jump."

"I'll go first," Eddie volunteered.

"No," said the Giant. "I've been thinking about that, too. Now that it is dark, Beni must go first each time."

"Why?" Eddie asked.

"Because of Trogs," said Marques.

Eddie didn't understand Marques's answer, but he certainly didn't feel a need to argue if it involved Trogs. "Girls first," he said gallantly.

The Giant lowered Beni a few feet below the lower ledge. Then he began to swing her slowly, arcing her toward the lower ledge. She held the rope tightly the first time she swung over it, but on the second pass she released her grip and landed safely.

Sandy went next. He, too, held onto the rope the first time it went over the ledge. He also held on the second and third time.

"Jump, Sandy, jump," yelled Beni.

"I can't," said Sandy on his fourth swing over.

"I'll have to try something different with him," said Marques to Eddie.

On Sandy's sixth pass, Marques did try something different. He gave a stronger swing, then he let about five feet of the rope slide through his hands before regripping it. With the extra length, Sandy came down squarely on the ledge. Beni, Eddie and Marques immediately broke out in laughter.

"Ow," yelled Sandy. "Be a little more gentle, you big brute. And stop laughin'; it wasn't at all funny."

"It sure looked funny," Eddie said to the laughing Giant.

"Maybe next time you'll jump," Marques yelled down. Turning to Eddie, Marques said, "Your turn. And I don't have to tell you to jump, do I?"

"Don't worry, I'll jump," said Eddie as Marques lowered him. Eddie descended to the distance the others had and then he stopped for an instant while the Giant adjusted himself to swing Eddie back and forth.

"Look out!" yelled Beni just as Eddie had begun his swing.

Suddenly Eddie was jerked out of the graceful motion and sent colliding into the face of the canyon.

"Ouch," Eddie cried out. Above he heard a blood-curdling shriek. Eddie would have recognized that sound anywhere; he had heard it once before, on Big Mountain, and he had hoped never to hear it again—it was the growl of a Trog.

Eddie looked up. Marques no longer looked down; instead, he lay on his back. With his right hand he still held the rope; with his left hand he held the ramlike horn of the devilish Trog.

The Trog growled and clawed at Marques. Still, Marques held onto the rope. The Giant extended his left arm in an effort to fend off the Trog. While struggling with the Trog one-handed, Marques began sweeping his rope arm to and fro. As he did so, Eddie began to move in an arc, watching the lower ledge to time his jump. On his first pass, he let go and landed half off the ledge. He groped for something solid to pull himself up, but only slipped farther down. Just as he thought he would fall, both Beni and Sandy grabbed an arm. Struggling, they pulled him up onto the ledge.

On the ledge above, Marques now had both hands on the Trog's horns and lifted the nasty creature by them. Mighty Marques grunted, twisted at the waist and heaved the Trog away from the canyon's face. Eddie watched the Trog fall until darkness consumed it. Then he raised his eyes upward to the Giant.

"Are you all right?" asked Eddie.

"Never felt better," said the Giant. Undaunted, Marques merely picked up the rope and tossed it to the lower ledge. Then he swung his body down and gripped rocks protruding from the canyon's edge. It was too far to jump, so he slowly climbed across the sheer cliff to the others. When he got to them, he looked exhausted.

"Are you sure you're all right?" asked Eddie.

"So maybe I have felt better," said Marques, "but I'm fine."

Marques had definitely looked better. He was badly scratched and his face, neck and arms were bleeding. Beni attended to the Giant's wounds with Sandy's help. Marques, Eddie knew, was important to them—even wounded he was stronger than the rest of them combined.

"He'll be okay," said Beni. Eddie breathed a sigh of relief.

Noticing a cave on their ledge, Eddie turned away. Something in the center of the Canyon of Death caught his eye. He squinted. A strange, thin rock formation rose about two-thirds up the height of the canyon. Resting on top of it was a jet-black fortress.

"What's that?" asked Eddie, pointing to the shiny black object.

"That," said Beni, "is Dark Castle."

"Mortimer's home," added Sandy as if Eddie might have forgotten.

The castle looked too frightening to be anybody's home—even Mortimer's. Its imposing air made Eddie—and probably every other visitor who had ever seen it—feel unwelcome. Every ounce of muscle in Eddie wanted to turn around and run, but there was nowhere to run to. Eddie knew that with Mortimer's castle in view, he was now truly in danger—as if the danger of Trogs was not enough.

Marques picked up the rope and said, "Let's keep going, shall we?"

He walked to both ends of the ledge and concluded, "This one's easy. There's a ledge straight below us."

Eddie walked toward the far end where Marques stood, glanced down, but could not even see another ledge. All he saw was one long, treacherous drop.

"Not this side; the other one," said Marques.

Eddie followed Marques to the other side. There, he stopped in front of a cave and peered over the edge. Straight below them, about ten feet down, part of a ledge stuck out in plain view. Getting to it would be easy enough.

The Giant lowered the rope. Beni climbed down. Almost immediately the other three heard her scream. Looking down, Eddie watched Beni back up and heard the shriek of a Trog.

The animal came into view, hoofing toward Beni. From above, Eddie could see its curved horns and smell its foul stench. Beni retreated to the edge of her ledge, still screaming. The Trog shrieked its heinous shriek and, extending its hairy arms, exposed long, sharp claws on each hand. It stepped toward Beni.

"Beni, use your power," Marques yelled down.

Suddenly Beni stopped screaming. She cupped both of her hands in front of her and, in an instant, her hands filled with fire, flooding the whole ledge with light. The light gave Eddie his first good look at a Trog. And it was more frightening than Eddie had imagined. The creature's face slightly resembled a gorilla's, but was more menacing. It had angry eyes and a wide nostril. Its growl revealed teeth, sharp and fanged. Blinded by the light, the Trog screamed in pain and covered its blood-red eyes with its hairy arms. Eddie could see the sharp claws as the beast backed away from Beni.

Beni tossed the flame at the creature, causing it to screech wildly.

"It went inside a cave," she said triumphantly.

"You'll both be safer down there," said Marques.

"Quite right," Sandy agreed as he began climbing down the rope.

"Now I understand why you wanted Beni to go first," Eddie said to Marques. Instead of getting a response from the Giant, Marques shoved Eddie toward the center of the ledge. Turning, Eddie saw why. A Trog lunged from the cave next to where Eddie had been standing. Marques backed away from the Trog, keeping Eddie behind him. Then a second Trog appeared from the same cave.

"Stay near the face of the wall, Eddie," Marques whispered while guiding Eddie toward the wall. Marques stayed in the center of the ledge, staring down the beasts.

Eddie watched as one of the Trogs began digging its heel into the ground in the same motion that a bull would make just before it was about to charge. The first Trog lowered its horns and did charge—right at Marques. It looked to Eddie as if Marques tackled the Trog. His big friend grabbed the horns as they struck his chest and fell on top of the Trog at the edge of the ledge—the edge with the drop off. He held it face down as the beast's breath kicked up the dirt underneath its face. Marques, who was on his knees, struggled with the animal, trying to push it into the void.

While Marques dragged the one Trog partially off the ledge, the other growled, scraped its heel, lowered its horns and also charged him. Eddie screamed. Marques, holding the Trog right at the edge, tried to get up. But he couldn't get to his feet in time. The Trog hit Marques squarely and the Giant fell backwards, off the ledge; as he fell he grabbed the horn of the charging beast with his right hand. Held by the horn, the Trog flew off its feet and fell after Marques.

Marques had tried to take both Trogs with him, but the one he had pinned down remained. Eddie wanted to run over to where his friend had fallen, but the remaining Trog shook itself and sprang to its feet about five steps in front of Eddie. It growled its evil growl and began to scrape its hoof.

Eddie felt the end was near. His giant protector had fallen off the ledge; his wizard friend stood on the ledge below with his trusted escort. Eddie closed his eyes in fear as the Trog began its charge. Just then, the ledge that Eddie and the Trog stood on began to shake and split. Eddie opened his eyes in wonder. The ledge had divided into four sections and Eddie stood on the smallest of the four, in the middle of the ledge. As the

charging Trog reached the section adjacent to Eddie's small slice, something miraculous happened. That section crumbled to bits and the Trog fell through the crumbling stone to the tune of his own hair-raising scream.

But then something uncomfortably strange happened. Eddie's section began to descend, slowly at first and then more quickly. He sped past the ledge Sandy and Beni were on, just out of their reach. Soaring down the face of the Canyon of Death as if he were riding an out-of-control elevator, Eddie began to scream. He had that awful sensation of falling; that sensation that, right as you fall asleep, wakes you up. Only Eddie was already awake; so he screamed and screamed again.

Suddenly his piece of rock hit the bottom of the canyon, but instead of breaking into a thousand pieces as Eddie expected, it continued to glide along the floor of the canyon toward the center. Now Eddie had the feeling that he was riding a runaway skateboard, and although this feeling was a lot more fun, Eddie was still scared. He was surprised that he was not thrown from the rock. It seemed that every time he thought he would lose his balance some remarkable force held him up.

Eddie began to realize that he was heading straight toward the towering rock holding Dark Castle. Almost as soon as he realized it, he reached it. He expected to be thrown against the huge rock formation in a sudden stop, but instead, without hesitation or change of speed, he began climbing the steep face.

Up, up and up Eddie soared at an incredible speed until he reached the top of the giant rock and could see the front of the imposing black structure that was Dark Castle. But his rock did not stop. It moved right toward Dark Castle. As it neared the castle, a hidden sliding double door opened. He sped through this door and into the confines of the castle. Then the rock ride stopped.

Eddie found himself in a black room in front of a big black chair, looking right at Mortimer.

"Welcome, I've been expecting you," said Mortimer as he threw back his head and laughed his evil laugh.

15

DARK CASTLE

Eddie stood on his rock, trembling in front of the evil warlock. From less than three feet away, Mortimer sneered at him.

The warlock spread out his arms. His shiny black robe drooped down, making him appear larger and, at the same time, much more menacing. "This is my royal throne room. Beautiful, isn't it?"

Eddie wasn't sure how to answer: The room certainly wasn't beautiful, but he didn't want to anger its owner, so he just stood there staring at the evil man.

"Leaves you speechless, does it?" Mortimer asked as he put his hands on the armrests of his throne. The pale gray of his skin stood out sharply against the black of the robe and of the room.

Eddie looked at Mortimer's filthy fingernails. Then the boy took in Mortimer's horrible, ashen face—the long and crooked nose; the small, black eyes centered within blood-shot circles; the plastered-down, black hair which came to a sharp point at the forehead. Worse even than his appearance was the foul odor which Mortimer's body emitted. He smelled like death itself. Eddie truly wished himself elsewhere.

Suddenly, Mortimer stood up and said, "Follow me!" He walked across the room to the far corner. Mortimer turned and saw that Eddie had not followed.

"You *will* follow me," Mortimer said. But fear pinned Eddie onto his little rock. "If not by your choice, then by mine shall you come."

Then Mortimer stretched both arms out toward Eddie. Squinting with one eye and glaring with the other, the rancid one pulled his right arm toward his chest: Eddie's left leg moved forward. Then Mortimer moved his right hand back out while he pulled his left toward his chest, and Eddie's right leg simultaneously stepped toward Mortimer. Against his will, Eddie moved forward. Mortimer threw his head back laughing with evil pleasure while Eddie's body responded like a stiff-legged robot.

"Fun, isn't it?" Mortimer said when Eddie was not quite half-way to him. "But it's not fast enough."

Mortimer reached out toward Eddie, turned his palms upward and raised them. Eddie rose a good foot off the ground. Dismayed, Eddie found himself completely unable to bring himself back to the floor. Mortimer brought his arms in and Eddie sped through the air toward him, stopping mere inches from his face.

Mortimer leaned even closer to Eddie—so close Eddie could smell his foul breath. His spit hit Eddie's face as he spoke. "Next time I expect you to do as I say. Understand?" Eddie nodded. "Good."

Then Mortimer did something that made Eddie's skin crawl: He put a hand on Eddie's shoulder. With it, he lowered Eddie back down to the floor. The boy tried to pull away from him, but Mortimer kept his hand on Eddie's shoulder. Turning to face the wall behind him, Mortimer flicked his free hand at the wall. A section of it slid open in front of them. Eddie was amazed, for there had been no sign whatsoever of a door. Mortimer pushed Eddie through the opening. As quickly as it had opened, the hidden door slid shut behind them. They stood in front of a long, dark staircase which spiraled upward as far as Eddie could see.

"Follow me to the top of the stairs," Mortimer commanded.

Mortimer began climbing the stairs and Eddie reluctantly followed; he preferred walking under his own power to being forcibly pulled along. Mortimer, noticing that Eddie followed of his own accord, flashed an evil grin. They walked up and up, circling round and round. The staircase, to Eddie, seemed like an unending spiral. When he dared look down the center, he could not see the bottom. When they did reach the top, they stood on a large, square step bordered by a solid wall on three sides.

"Where do you suppose the door is?" asked Mortimer.

Eddie pointed straight in front of him.

Mortimer waved his hand and a door slid open where Eddie had pointed. It appeared to lead into another dreary looking room, but when Eddie tried to enter it Mortimer stopped him.

"Fool!" said Mortimer. "Yet that is how every fool is meant to act. What you see is not what is there."

Mortimer spun his hand around and, like a magician, produced a large rock. He tossed the rock into the room. Eddie watched the rock fall toward the floor, but when it reached the floor it fell through it. Suddenly the room in front of them vanished. Instead of opening to a room, this door opened to the outside, way up near the top of Dark Castle. The door, extending over the rock formation, created a drop that went down to the floor of the Canyon of Death. Eddie leaned over and watched the rock fall into the darkness of the canyon.

"Doors where there are no doors. Rooms where there are no rooms. Such clever defenses protect me from unwanted visitors. Neither of your pint-sized friends will stand a chance, you can be certain of that. You should have chosen your companions with greater care. Dark Castle would have been too difficult to enter even for your Giant, had he lived."

Eddie, reminded of Marques's fall, began to cry. Instinctively he felt that Marques would have had the best chance of helping. Eddie did not feel selfish pity over his predicament; he felt genuine sorrow. For Marques had been not only a loyal and valuable companion but a true friend. And even though Eddie had seen the Giant fall, he could not believe—or did not want to believe—that Marques was dead.

Even while his mind dwelled on the sorrow, another disturbing thought forced itself foremost in his mind. "How did you know about Marques's fall? And how did you know we were even here?"

"How? Yes, how indeed. And how is it that you have ended your silence? Agreeing to be civil and to talk with me, are you? Well, I'll do better than tell you how, I'll show you how. Seeing is believing, they say. Your answer awaits through this door."

Mortimer pointed to the right and the wall there slid open, revealing another room. Mortimer and Eddie entered it and the wall slid closed behind them.

This room was about the same size as Eddie's bedroom, but there the similarity ended. The floor had square black cobblestones. In the center of the room a black slab, resembling an operating table, rested on two wide black legs. A solid black wall lined three sides of the room, but the fourth wall was much different.

Mortimer pointed to that wall and spit, "There is your answer."

On that far wall a whole series of crystal balls were placed in rows and columns of six.

"This is my monitoring room."

Mortimer led Eddie closer to the crystal balls. As Eddie approached them, he saw that each held a holographic image of the Canyon of Death.

"There are your two remaining friends," Mortimer said, pointing to one of the crystals. In it, Eddie saw Beni and Sandy huddled together, near a fire, on the same ledge he had last seen them on. Three Trogs stood with them, but they stood just out of the flame's light.

"We shall see how long your young wizard can hold out," Mortimer said. "Her spell, although a simple one, is draining. She won't be able to maintain it much longer. So we shall soon see your last two friends eaten by Trogs."

Eddie shook with fright at the thought. Mortimer merely chuckled.

"Shall we hear them?" asked Mortimer.

"You could hear us, too?" asked Eddie in disbelief.

"But of course," said Mortimer. "I like to stay on top of things. Especially things as essential to me as your imagination—I mean, *my* imagination." Mortimer again laughed. Then he turned a knob at the bottom of the crystal ball, filling the room with the sound of growling Trogs.

"Ah, music to my ears," said Mortimer. "The only better sound they make comes when they rip apart their prey. And the sight of them eating! I thoroughly enjoy watching that. Maybe I should help it along? I can easily extinguish her flame."

Eddie shook his head, but Mortimer brought his hand over the crystal ball and rubbed his thumb across his four fingers in the motion of a chef adding spices to his dish. The flame instantly went out. Mortimer laughed.

"No!" cried Eddie.

"Not again," Beni said.

Eddie heard her as if she were in the room with him. Watching the crystal, Eddie saw the Trogs move toward Beni and Sandy, but Beni again hurled flames at them.

"Keep them away, lass," said Sandy. "Do you think you can get another fire goin'?"

"I hope so," said Beni. "But I do feel very tired. I don't know if I can keep this up much longer."

Beni circled her arms and a big flame blazed up. And as it did, the Trogs backed away from the pair.

"Good job!" said Eddie, but his friends could not hear him.

"Boring," said Mortimer, covering a yawn with his hand. "Trust me, though, it will get more interesting later. Enough of these for now." Mortimer waved his arms toward the crystal balls and the scenes on them changed dramatically.

The first row filled with six different views of Sandsibar: The first crystal in that row showed Sleepy Cove, where even now

Sandmen harvested their special sleeping sand; the second showed Town Square; the third, Sand Castle; the fourth, the harbor where Eddie had received his boat; the fifth and sixth revealed unfamiliar parts of the island.

Dire Straits could be seen in the second row of crystals, with the flying sharks plainly in view on the fourth ball in that row. Big Mountain filled the third row. The fourth revealed parts of the Poisoned River and the Valley of Giants. The fifth row held scenes of the Deserted Desert starting with the waterfall hiding Beni's cave and ending with the Canyon of Death. Sandy and Beni were visible on the last crystal of that row. The last row of crystals showed a part of Dreamland which Eddie hadn't seen and which resembled a jungle.

"These are not the crystals that interest me," said Mortimer. "Nor should they be the ones that interest you. I think you'll find this next one much more to your liking."

Eddie did not at all like Mortimer's tone. He became more apprehensive, keeping his eyes on Mortimer, who walked to the foot of the black-slabbed table. There, the floor opened, leaving a large square hole. A crystal ball, triple the size of the others, rose from the hole on a black pillar, which stopped when it rose to the height of the table.

"Look into this ball," said Mortimer.

Eddie did. But as he did, he could not believe what he saw. For in that crystal ball, Eddie saw himself. And not like he would have seen himself in a mirror. He saw himself in another place, doing something entirely different—and much more desirable. He saw himself sound asleep in his own bed.

"That can't be," said Eddie in dismay.

"Yet it is. In the Real World, your body lives and breathes and sleeps. Unfortunately for you, you are not dreaming, as most little boys would be. Fortunately for me, you are in Dreamland wide awake. But remember, you are not fully here. Only your essence—my imagination—is here."

"What about me?" asked Eddie.

"What about you?" said Mortimer. "You will merely cease to exist as soon as someone from the Real World attempts to wake you up. At that fortuitous moment your imagination shall be all mine!"

"No!" Eddie yelled.

"You shall see, it shall be." Mortimer walked past the foot of the table. He clapped his hands and a portion of the wall slid up, exposing two clocks. One, with a plaque reading "Dreamland" under it, showed five after four; the other had a plaque which read "Real World" and showed six thirty-five.

"Let's see," said Mortimer, "you have been in Dreamland for forty-six hours our time. That amounts to, uh, about six and a half hours your time. You left the Real World at precisely midnight. As you see, this clock has the time in the Real World. It is now a little after six thirty in the morning your time. That clock shows the time here in Dreamland. You arrived at six in the morning on your first day in Dreamland. So when our clock shows seven, you will have been here forty-nine hours our time—and seven yours. That means both clocks will have precisely the same time. When both clocks show seven, I will cast a spell on them which can only be cast when time stands equal in both worlds. It is called the Clock Lock, and it will speed up Dreamland time by seven. Do you understand?"

Eddie really didn't. Mortimer's explanation had his head spinning, but he did realize that the news was bad.

"It means less time for you. Dreamland's time will equal the Real World's time for a period of seven hours. See?" Eddie shook his head. "Never mind, then. Just tell me what time you usually get up."

"On Saturdays I usually sleep in till eight."

"Splendid!" said Mortimer. "Then it means once it is seven in both worlds, instead of waiting seven hours, I shall wait but one!"

Now Eddie understood the horror. His time would run out seven times faster. He glanced back to the monitoring crystals for another look at his friends. They were his only hope. Again, he thought of Marques. "Where did Marques land?"

"What?" His question took Mortimer by surprise.

"When Marques fell, where did he land?"

"I don't know. I didn't see him land," said Mortimer. "I had to make sure that nothing happened to my imagination. I had to save you from the Trogs. You should thank me for that."

"How do you know he's dead?" asked Eddie.

"What?" said Mortimer. "You saw the drop. I did not need to see him land to know that wherever he landed was too far down to survive."

But Mortimer seemed to harbor doubts, for he turned toward his thirty-six crystal monitoring system and flicked his hands at them. Again, all thirty-six crystals showed the Canyon of Death. The scenes quickly changed until Mortimer found exactly what he was looking for.

"There is your Giant," he said, relieved.

Lying on a ledge, crumpled over the Trog he had taken with him, was Marques. A tear came to Eddie's eye.

"Enough of your foolish thoughts!" Mortimer said. "My plans have worked perfectly so far. Now I must attend to some last-minute details for the Imagination Transformation. It will soon be all over for you. In the meantime, I might as well let you watch and listen while your friends get eaten by Trogs."

Mortimer turned on the sound under Sandy and Beni's crystal.

"Enjoy!" he said, walking through the hidden passageway. The door slid shut behind him, leaving Eddie alone. Once more Eddie looked at Marques lying motionless and cried. Then he looked at Beni and Sandy. Eddie watched the rows of crystals and prayed his two remaining friends would find a way to save him.

16

THE ROWS
OF CRYSTALS

Left alone in Mortimer's monitoring room, Eddie could only wait—and watch. Beni and Sandy huddled near her dying flame while three Trogs stood outside the circle of light. Eddie was thankful that Mortimer left the sound on. Despite the unpleasant Trog noises, having the sound on comforted Eddie. He felt closer to his friends and less alone.

But Eddie also realized that hope was running out as the clocks advanced. So he kept a good eye on the time as well. When it was nearly five in Dreamland, Eddie heard Beni speak.

"I don't think I can hold on much longer."

"You have to, lass."

"I'm getting really tired, Sandy. Even if we do get to poor Eddie in time, I doubt that I can be of any help. Making Mortimer powerless involves a difficult Dispel Spell— and it must be spoken word for word. I don't have it memorized and my *Book of Spells* is in Marques's backpack. Oh, poor Marques."

"He was quite a hero, that one," said Sandy. "I never knew I could care so much for a Giant, but Mighty Marques was the kind of stock that legends are made of."

Again the two were silent. A few minutes later Beni spoke again.

"I don't know how long the Dispel Spell will last, or even how long it takes for it to make your sand good. And I can't cast the Dispel Spell without my wand. Heaven only knows where Mortimer has that."

"The wand!" whispered Eddie to himself. He had nearly forgotten about it. He searched the room for it while his friends continued talking. He could find no secret compartments and no wand.

"And how are we to get down with the rope still on the ledge above us? I'm afraid Eddie was right about me—I'm not much of a wizard at all," Beni said forlornly.

"No," yelled Eddie, "I was wrong— you're a great wizard."

But neither Sandy nor Beni could hear Eddie.

"Now, now," Sandy said consolingly, "you're bein' too hard on yerself, lass."

"I can't keep the fire going," Beni said, watching it flicker lamely. "I'm all burned out."

"What other spells can you do?" asked Sandy.

"Just the other half of the Fire and Ice spell."

The three Trogs growled loudly, sensing feeding time was near. They started toward Sandy and Beni as the fire began to wither.

"Can you make a large piece of ice?" Sandy asked urgently.

"Sure, but I don't see—" Beni's expression changed. "Oh, yes, I do see."

Beni stood up with a renewed vigor. Thrusting forward her arms, a large piece of ice formed between the pair and the Trogs. The ice filled up the whole depth of the ledge, rising as high as the ledge above, and blocked the passage of the Trogs. It intensified the dying fire, sending out a brilliant light which caused the Trogs to writhe in pain. Eddie watched in the crystal ball as the Trogs backed up; one Trog plummeted off the ledge. The others headed back inside the cave.

"Phew," sighed Beni, "Now I can relax until the ice melts."

"I think not, lass," said Sandy. "We must figure out a way to get the rope."

197

As they glanced overhead, Eddie, too, looked above them. When Marques had pushed Eddie away from the Trog—saving Eddie's life—he had pulled the rope upward. Now it dangled just over the upper ledge well above Sandy and Beni.

"Oh, it's useless, Sandy. Even when I stood on your shoulders, it was out of reach. We've already tried everything we could think of."

"True," said Sandy. "So we'll just have to think of somethin' else. How I wish Marques or Eddie were with us, for one of them surely would've had an idea."

Both sat down, thinking. A few minutes later, Beni stood up. "I've got an idea that I think might work, Sandy." Using fire, she began to melt steps into the block of ice, making a makeshift ladder.

"Lassie, I think you've done it!" Sandy easily climbed to the top and grabbed the rope. "We can work our way down now. Yer idea, lass, was worthy of Marques."

Reminded again of the gentle Giant, Eddie glanced down to the third crystal in the fifth row to see Marques.

"Oh, Marques," said Eddie, "why did you have to die?"

Yet even as he said this, something truly remarkable happened—something so completely defying belief that Eddie thought he must be dreaming. For inside the third crystal of the fifth row there was a sign of life. It seemed to Eddie that Marques had moved his head. But he was suddenly still again. Just as Eddie had convinced himself that he must have been wrong, Marques moved once more.

Marques was alive!

"Wow!" exclaimed Eddie. By whatever miracle, Marques had survived a fall that no Sandman or human, let alone another Giant, could have.

Although Eddie heard Beni and Sandy talking, his eyes remained fixed on Marques. Eddie reached for the sound knob below the third crystal and turned it up.

The Giant rubbed his hand across his forehead and groaned as though he had a terrible headache (which, of course, he must have had). He sat up and appeared dazed. Looking lost and confused, he sat for quite some time staring at the dead Trog next to him before his mind cleared. Then, remembering everything, he said but one word: "Eddie!"

The Giant sprang to his feet and looked around. Already dawn was breaking inside the Canyon of Death bringing by degrees the light of day.

"I hope it's not too late!" said the Giant. Cupping his hands, he yelled, "Eddie! Beni! Sandy!"

The canyon echoed these three names over and over so loudly that Eddie felt certain he would have heard it even if the crystal's sound were not on. And he worried that Mortimer might have heard it as well.

Thinking of Mortimer, Eddie glanced at the clocks. It was exactly five-thirty-six in Dreamland and twelve minutes to seven in the Real World.

"Didcha hear somethin', lass?" Sandy's question made Eddie relax a little. Maybe the yell hadn't been quite as loud as it seemed.

"It sure sounded like Marques," said Beni.

"It must be one of Mortimer's rotten tricks," Sandy said sharply.

"I don't think so," said Beni. "I have a feeling that Mortimer won't concern himself with us as long as he has Eddie."

"Sounds logical enough," said Sandy.

Beni cupped her hands and yelled, "We're up here!"

We're up here, we're up here, we're up here, echoed through the Canyon of Death. Again Eddie worried that Mortimer would hear.

Whether or not the evil warlock heard, Mighty Marques certainly had. He swung his body around and, with great difficulty, began climbing the face of the canyon. Eddie watched as first his head, then torso, and finally his legs disappeared from view as Marques climbed out of the crystal's range. Although Eddie could no longer see the Giant, he was thrilled with the knowledge that Marques was alive.

Not long afterwards, Eddie heard Sandy exclaim, "Well, I'll be, if it isn't Mighty Marques!"

Sandy was looking down from his ledge, and although Eddie couldn't see below it, he knew Marques must be nearby. Marques's arm suddenly came into view, and then his head and his body, as he pulled himself onto the ledge.

"Me goodness, man, we thoughtcha were dead." Sandy danced a little jig as he said this.

"Indeed," said an exhausted Giant, "I thought so myself."

"What happened?" asked Beni, "How did you survive it?"

"Yeah, how?" asked Eddie, quite forgetting the others couldn't hear him.

"I don't know how," Marques said to Beni. "All I know is I fell down very far and very fast. I tried to swing the Trog outward away from me, but it grabbed tightly onto me. I ended up falling right on top of it. The Trog broke my fall. That must have saved my life. Still, I must confess that I was knocked unconscious clear up until I yelled for you.

However long that was, I couldn't say. . . . Hey, where is Eddie?"

The others filled the Giant in on what had happened to Eddie. Marques was obviously discouraged by the news.

"My poor little friend," the Giant said, shaking his head. "We must save him."

"Let's do it," said Sandy, handing Marques the rope.

"We must get down as quickly as possible," said Marques. "Since the light is out, we no longer have to worry about Trogs. I'll lower this rope as far as it will go and we'll see how close to the ground we can get."

Eddie watched while the Giant fed more and more rope down.

"Okay," said Marques, "you two climb down it while I hold it. Then I'll drop it and climb down after you."

Eddie watched while first Sandy and then Beni climbed out of his view. Marques then released the rope, got on his knees, grabbed the ledge and lowered himself. He, too, vanished from the crystal. Eddie now watched a monitoring system that showed him nothing he wanted to see. Each crystal held parts of the canyon, but each scene was perfectly still. Eddie glanced back and forth from the two big clocks to the six rows of crystals.

He waited. And waited. And waited.
Finally, at six-forty in Dreamland—and about
three minutes to seven in the Real World—
Eddie again saw his friends. They came into
view in the second crystal of the sixth row.
Their movement caught Eddie's attention.
That crystal showed the foot of the large rock
formation under Dark Castle.

Eddie turned the volume up.

"It will be impossible for the girl and I to
climb up, I'm afraid," said Sandy.

Marques paced back and forth, tapping
his chin with his index finger.

"I have an idea," he said at last. He
grabbed the huge rope near its center. With his
hands about three feet apart, he lifted the rope
over his head and lowered it behind his back.
Then he crossed his arms in front of him at his
waist, so that the rope encircled him. "Now I
shall tie an end securely around each of you." He
tied one end firmly around Beni and the other
around Sandy. "I will climb the rock. You two
will follow behind me. I'll support your weight
and do the climbing, but you must help me by
walking along the face of the rock. Got it?"

Beni and Sandy nodded. Marques began
to climb up. Soon, he climbed out of Eddie's
view. Shortly thereafter, the rope became taut,
and Sandy and Beni took their first steps upon

the rock, holding onto the rope above the knot that Marques had made.

Just then, Eddie heard a sound within the monitoring room and spun around. The unseen door through which Mortimer had left had slid open. Eddie's heart quickened as the dark-clad warlock walked into the room. But Eddie's mind also worked quickly: The sixth row of crystals was just above Eddie's waist, so he stood in front of the crystal which showed his friends, blocking Mortimer's view. Then he reached behind his back and turned the sound down on that ball.

Mortimer, wearing an evil grin, looked completely pleased with himself. He did not appear to suspect anything. (But Eddie's demeanor would soon change that, for the expression of a child with something to hide is all too revealing.)

Mortimer glanced at the crystal ball where Beni and Sandy were when he had left the room. "Your friends are gone I see," he said. "Were they eaten by the Trogs?"

"Yes, it was terrible."

"And you, my foolish child, are a terrible liar," said the witch. "What are you hiding?"

"Nothing," said Eddie. Mortimer pushed him aside and Eddie nearly panicked. But the crystal he was hiding showed no signs of his friends; they had had enough time to climb out of its range.

Mortimer still looked suspicious, but having no basis for his suspicions, soon turned away. "Everything is in place," said the evil one. "It is nearly time for the Clock Lock. But first, you must get on the table."

Mortimer pointed to the black slab in the middle of the room. Eddie shook his head. He had no intention of getting on that table.

"If you don't get on the table, I'll get you on the table."

Still Eddie refused.

"Have it your way, then," said Mortimer as he raised his hands, pulling Eddie off the ground. Then Mortimer spun his hands, causing Eddie to spin face down toward the floor and turn completely upside down before finally stopping, flat on his back in midair, with a view of the ceiling. Mortimer moved Eddie over the black slab and lowered him onto it. Clasps immediately wrapped over his body. He had a strap across his chest, waist and thighs as well as one across each wrist and ankle. They were so tight that Eddie could hardly move at all.

Mortimer glared at the clocks. Seven to seven was the time in Dreamland; one minute to seven the time in the Real World. "Now I must attend to the Clock Lock. In the meantime, don't go anywhere." He laughed hysterically, as if Eddie going anywhere were the best joke he'd heard in years.

17

THE CLOCK LOCK

Mortimer opened a hidden compartment. He pulled out a desktop from under the clocks in the same fashion that Eddie's mom would pull out her cutting board in the kitchen. Then he opened a hidden drawer. Mortimer lifted a *Book of Spells* from the drawer and set it on the desk. He flipped through the book until he came to the Clock Lock spell. Once he found it, he reached back into the drawer, pulling out Beni's wand—Eddie's heart jumped!

Eddie glanced from the wand to the clocks. One minute to seven, Dreamland time—just seconds away from seven in the Real World. Mortimer appeared calm, as though the passing time meant nothing to him.

When there were but fourteen seconds left in Dreamland—and but two in the Real World—Mortimer raised the wand and began to chant the spell.

> *Time approaching toward like hours*
> *Finds itself within my powers:*
> *Dreamland creatures speed your talking*
> *Clocks in realms unlike are locking.*

Mortimer finished precisely as each clock hit seven. Eddie felt an instantaneous jolt, as if an earthquake had hit. Then everything returned to normal—except for the clocks. The two clocks, which had been moving at different speeds the whole of Eddie's stay, suddenly moved in unison. Mortimer laughed delightedly. His spell had worked.

"Now, my young friend, your fate is nearly sealed. All that remains is the Imagination Transformation. When someone from the Real World tries to wake you, it will be all over for you!"

Mortimer glanced at the rows of crystals. Fearing for his friends, Eddie also turned his head toward the crystals. His friends were nowhere to be seen; Mortimer had another motive.

"Speaking of the Real World," Mortimer said, "it's time to change the channels." Mortimer snapped his fingers and all thirty-six

crystal balls changed. The new views startled Eddie. Each crystal revealed a different section of Eddie's home. In one crystal his dad was reading the newspaper at the kitchen table; in another, his mom was cooking bacon and eggs in the kitchen; in yet another, Eddie himself slept soundly—just as he did in the large crystal at the foot of the table.

"Would you like sound?" said Mortimer. "Of course you would."

Another snap of the fingers and Eddie could hear the sizzling of the bacon in the kitchen.

Then Eddie heard his mother: "Breakfast is almost ready, dear."

"It smells great," said his father.

Tears rolled down Eddie's cheeks as he saw and heard the two people he loved most in all the world. He watched as his mom and dad continued to have a normal morning conversation, oblivious to the perils their young son faced.

"Did Eddie enjoy the game?"

"He loved it. The Giants really beat up on the Dodgers. Eddie was thrilled."

"I bet he loves the baseball cards, too."

"Looked at them all the way home."

Imitating Eddie, his mom's eyes grew wide and she said, "Wow!" Both his parents shared a laugh.

"Yes sir, he thought it was something else all right," his father agreed.

Mortimer broke in, turning down the sound. "They're likely to go on like this for some time. Their idle chatter is of no interest. When they go to wake you, now *that* will be of interest."

Suddenly a flashing red light broke the room's blackness and an electronic voice droned, "Red alert."

"Intruders?" Mortimer said incredulously as he instantly changed the crystals from scenes of the Real World to scenes of Dark Castle. Once he had changed the crystals, the red light and the strange voice both stopped.

The rows of crystals now showed interior and exterior views of Dark Castle—one even showed Eddie and Mortimer looking into the crystals. That crystal was not the one that attracted Mortimer's attention; he was looking at the one that showed Sandy, Beni and Marques outside of Dark Castle.

"So . . . the Giant did not die. You were convinced, having seen him fall, that he might still be alive. I, seeing the same thing, was convinced of his death. What a relief it will be to have an imagination and imagine the possibilities that I ignore."

Mortimer turned up the sound. Eddie heard the impact as Marques pounded against the outside wall of Dark Castle. The Giant took a running start and powered his shoulder full force against the wall. Nothing budged.

"Look at the clouds," said Sandy. "Either me eyes are playin' tricks or those clouds are speedin' across the sky."

"Your eyes are fine, Sandy," Beni said. "That quake we felt must have been the Clock Lock."

"What's that?" asked Sandy.

"A spell to speed up time by a factor of seven."

"Oh," said Sandy.

"We must really hurry now," said Beni. "We don't have much time left."

Again Marques squared his weight into the wall; again nothing happened.

"The fool!" said Mortimer. "With all of his strength, let alone half, his attempt would be futile. We need not concern ourselves with them. We must complete the preparation for the Imagination Transformation."

Mortimer raised his hand and flicked it; the rows of crystals returned to the Real World. Eddie's parents, both seated at the dining table, were eating breakfast.

Mortimer walked over to Eddie. He pulled out a black, plungerlike cap from the wall and secured it to the boy's head. Then Mortimer took out an identical cap and put it on his own head. The hats were connected by wires, which, in turn, ran to a red lever on the wall. Mortimer caressed that lever.

"When someone tries to wake you, I pull this switch and the Imagination Transformation takes place. I can't wait to have an imagination!"

"In all the time I've been in Dreamland," Eddie said timidly, "you're the only one who has shown any imagination whatsoever."

"You lie!" Mortimer said.

"No, I tell the truth," said Eddie. "Your whole scheme to get me to Dreamland was quite imaginative. Who else would have thought of tainting sleeping sand but you?"

"It's in the *Book of Spells* for all to see," said Mortimer.

"Oh, and flying sharks, that was imaginative—though far too scary for my liking. Trogs, too."

"Both found in the *Book of Spells*," said Mortimer.

"Then you poisoned a whole river and dried up a huge lake. You created a desert just so you'd have a place to live."

"All true," said Mortimer, gaining interest in Eddie's praise.

"To me the most remarkable thing of all is that you stopped a waterfall as it hit the ground. No one from the Real World has managed that—or imagined that. I think your imagination would be envied in the Real World."

"Really?" asked Mortimer, flattered.

"Really," said Eddie. "In fact, your imagination is superior to any I've known."

"How interesting!" said Mortimer with true delight.

"You have such a wonderful imagination that I seriously doubt you could use mine."

Mortimer's mood changed, "I should have known you'd have an ulterior motive for singing my praises. What you call my imagination is merely a casting of spells to create the result the spell intended. With a real imagination, my power will be beyond anything known in Dreamland—I shall create at will the results *I* desire. Your sweet talk will not dissuade me."

The blinking red light returned and with it the "Red alert" refrain.

"This is becoming a nuisance," said Mortimer, pulling the wired cap off of his head and again changing the crystals.

Eddie's friends had found the hidden door and the Giant had managed to move it an inch or two. His fingers were in the small slit, but he was obviously straining to keep it open.

"Let's hear what they're saying, shall we?" said Mortimer, turning up the volume.

"Come on, Marques, you can do it," urged Beni.

214

But the door proved to be too much even for Mighty Marques, who by now was a very tired and bruised Giant.

"I'm afraid I can't do it," sighed Marques.

"Don't get down on yourself," said Beni. "There must be some way of getting in."

"There is, lass!" said Sandy. "Remember how we got the rope down from the ledge above?"

"Sure," said Beni, "You merely climbed the ice ladder."

"And ice will open the door for us," said Sandy.

"What?" said Beni.

"Listen," said Sandy. "When Marques nudges the door open a crack, fill that crack with ice. Then make the ice wider and wider. But only make the ice a foot high, lass, so that we can climb over it."

Beni did what Sandy suggested. Sure enough, as the ice grew wider, it forced the door open. Eddie's three friends climbed over the ice to enter Dark Castle.

"Try as they might, they cannot help you," said Mortimer. "Still I don't like them getting in the way when the Transformation is so close at hand. I guess it's time I took care of your friends once and for all."

A black cloud rose in the monitoring room, on the crystal of the scene of the monitoring room and on the crystal showing the throne

215

room. When the smoke cleared, Mortimer had vanished from the one room and reappeared in the other. He stood before Eddie's friends.

"Fools," Mortimer said. "Did you really think you could save your pathetic little friend? You can't even begin to help without the wand." Mortimer pulled the wand out of his robe and held it high. "Besides, you are too late. Eddie's imagination is mine."

"If that is true," said Beni, "then give me the wand. You have no need of it any longer."

"The wand will be safely out of your reach," said Mortimer. He released the wand and, as it started to fall, it disappeared.

Eddie heard a noise and lifted his head. On the black podium, next to the large crystal, the wand appeared. It rocked back and forth as if dropped there, until it came to rest. Right next to the crystal showing Eddie asleep in the Real World, the wand which could save him lay.

"I knew you wouldn't give it to me," said an indignant Beni.

"What do you take me for?" said Mortimer, "I'm no fool. You three are all fools. And now I will kill all of you!"

Mortimer raised his arms, but before he could cast his evil spell, a blue light flashed in every room of Dark Castle. The blinking light was accompanied by an electronic voice that said, "Blue alert! Blue alert!"

216

Mortimer glanced nervously over his shoulder—in the direction of his hidden staircase. "A Real World alarm," he said under his breath. Strapped on the black slab, Eddie heard him. He glanced at the two clocks: It was about ten to eight.

"I shall deal with you three later," said Mortimer. "In the meantime, this should hold you."

He thrust his hand toward them and in an instant all three of Eddie's friends were smothered in shackles and chains. Mortimer disappeared into a black cloud, reappearing next to Eddie.

"Blue alert! Blue alert!" persisted the electronic voice.

Mortimer snapped his fingers, turning all crystals back to Eddie's home. He raised the sound. Then he placed the plunger-cap back on his head and readied his hand on the lever.

In one of the crystals, Eddie's mother was walking down the hall toward Eddie's room. Eddie and Mortimer both watched as she turned the knob of her son's door and gently opened it.

"This is what I've been waiting for!" shouted Mortimer. "The Imagination Transformation shall now commence!"

18

THE
IMAGINATION
TRANSFORMATION

Eddie watched the crystal as his mother peered into his room. To Eddie's immense relief, she immediately closed the door again.

Mortimer let out a curse. "How unreliable people from the Real World are!"

Eddie's mother rejoined his father, who sat in the living room.

"John," she said, obviously perturbed, "how could you let him go to sleep in his clothes?"

"Huh?" his father said, turning a page of the paper.

"You didn't make sure that he changed into his pajamas. Eddie slept in his clothes. John, are you listening to me?"

"Yes, dear, of course I am."

"Well, I'm supposed to take him to my mother's, you know, and if he's a grouch today—"

She left her statement hanging like a threat.

Eddie, though, heard the part that interested him. "Grandma's," he whispered. Going to Grandma's was one of his favorite things: She always had something special for him. His mother would occasionally take Eddie to Grandma's house to surprise him— and he certainly wasn't expecting it today.

"What time does he have to be up to get ready?" asked Eddie's dad.

"In about fifteen minutes."

Eddie's eyes grew wide—so did Mortimer's, but each for a different reason: Eddie's out of fear; Mortimer's from sheer delight.

The evil warlock wrung his hands excitedly. "The Clock Lock has already saved me valuable time."

Suddenly they were interrupted again as the red light flashed to the accompaniment of "Red Alert! Red Alert!"

"Now what!" said Mortimer, flicking the crystal balls back to Dark Castle. Eddie's eyes went to the last ball, where his friends had been chained. All that was left there were broken chains.

"Impossible!" Mortimer exclaimed.

Eddie's eyes scanned the crystal balls in search of his friends. They were still in the throne room. Marques was pounding against the area of the wall that hid the staircase. The evil wizard saw them, too, and turned up the volume.

"Are you certain Eddie's this way?" asked Sandy.

"As certain as I can be," said Marques. "When Mortimer was startled by the alarm, he looked over his shoulder in this direction."

Marques spoke his deductions while still pounding away.

"That Giant is too smart for his own good. I should have drained half his brain as well," said Mortimer. "But at least he won't be able to break through the wall."

Almost before the words were out of Mortimer's mouth, the wall gave way, revealing the hidden staircase.

"Impossible," said Mortimer again, but with less conviction. "It would have taken all of the Giant's strength to break that wall. *And* those chains. Yet I reduced his strength to half."

Eddie's expression changed, and Mortimer, noticing, drew the conclusion that Eddie had hoped to conceal.

"So, he has all of his strength," said Mortimer. "I must check the spell I cast."

Mortimer moved over to his *Book of Spells* at the desk and glanced through it. Eddie looked back to the crystals. His friends were climbing the spiral staircase at a good clip. Already they were about half-way up it.

"Ah," said Mortimer, "my spell reduced only his size, not his strength. It was a small oversight, one that shall be easy to remedy. I'll simply find a strength-reducing spell."

While Mortimer busied himself with his *Book of Spells*, Eddie watched his friends. When they reached the top of the stairs, Marques began looking for a door. He found the one to the room that wasn't there.

"No," said Eddie under his breath. He, too, had picked that door and he knew it was terribly wrong. Mustering all of his courage, Eddie yelled, "I'm in here!"

"No," said Mortimer, pointing to the crystal showing the nonexistent room "you're in there!"

Eddie heard his own voice yell "I'm in here!"—coming from that crystal.

"Hurry, Marques, he's in there," Eddie heard Beni shout.

"No," yelled Eddie as loud as he could.

"Foolish youth," Mortimer snapped back. "These walls are soundproof."

Indeed, Eddie could see that his warning had no effect, for Marques continued to struggle with the door. When he opened it at last, Eddie saw himself in that illusory room.

"Eddie!" Sandy yelled as he ran into the room.

But a terrible thing happened as Sandy crossed the threshold of that room. Just as the boulder Mortimer had thrown went through the floor, so, too, did Sandy. As he fell, the room vanished, showing once more that, in reality, this door opened to the outside of Dark Castle. Mortimer laughed, but stopped quickly: Sandy was luckier than the boulder had been. Marques, reacting instantly, had grabbed the little man by the arm as he fell. Soon Sandy was back on firm footing.

"Thankye, thankye," said the Sandman, glancing nervously out of the door.

"Now what?" said Beni.

Marques was pacing fist to chin, finger to cheek.

"There must be a door here somewhere," he said. "And we must find it."

All three began scouring the other two walls for it. Soon they found it. Marques slowly forced it open. As the Giant muscled open the door, Beni peered through the crack.

"He's in there," said Beni.

"It could be another trick," said Sandy warily.

Marques, though, continued to fight the door, inch by inch. He forced it open to the point where Beni and Sandy could fit through.

"Throw in one of your sandbags, Sandy," said Marques.

Sandy did so and determined the room was real. Sandy and Beni entered it.

"That Giant is more trouble to me than he's worth." Turning back to his *Book of Spells*, Mortimer said, "Ah, yes, here it is. The Maximum Strength Reducer." He coughed to clear his voice and incanted:

The strength that a Giant has in one hand,
Shall now be the strength in the whole of the man.

Just before the evil warlock finished the spell, Marques himself entered the room. But as soon as Mortimer spoke the last word, the Giant dropped to the floor. When Marques tried to get up, he found he could not.

Mortimer laughed, and Eddie thought he'd never heard a more insidious, insane laugh anywhere.

"You stupid fool," Mortimer addressed Marques. "I warned you not to help the boy. But did you listen? No! Now you shall pay with your life."

"No, it is you who shall pay with yours," said Beni. Her face showed determination.

Mortimer simply laughed at her. "You dare threaten *me*? Your power is no match for mine."

Mortimer flipped through his book looking for the proper spell with which to kill Marques. But Beni remained unperturbed. Holding out her arms, she produced fire in her left hand and ice in her right.

The flame caught Mortimer's attention and he looked up from his book just as Beni clapped her hands together with a thunderous clash. The sudden mix of fire and ice instantly produced a stream of water which flew right at Mortimer. Just as instantly, a black cloud rose where Mortimer had been and another rose on the other side of the room—where Mortimer reappeared.

"Clever," said Mortimer, "very clever, indeed. I had underestimated you. But it shall not happen again." With that, Mortimer flicked his wrist in Beni's direction.

"Yes, it will," said Beni. But when Beni thrust out her hands nothing happened. She looked at each, startled.

Mortimer laughed. "I have neutralized your only spell. Did you really think that you could stand up to me, the most powerful of all wizards? Fool that you were to think it." Mortimer walked around the table to face Eddie's friends. His tone turned deathly. "For interfering with my plans, you shall all die. I will start by killing you, Sandy. But your death will be quick and painless. After all, you did bring the boy to Dreamland. Then you, Beni, since you dare stand up to me. And since the Giant cannot stand up at all, he shall be the last to go." Mortimer laughed. Marques struggled in vain to lift his own weight. "Now where is your strength, Mighty Marques," said Mortimer with searing sarcasm as he stood above the fallen Giant. "I shall kill you *after* I have Eddie's imagination. Then I will be able to imagine the worst possible death with the most possible suffering." Mortimer leaned down, yanked Marques's hair and came face to face with the Giant. "It shall be the best possible revenge."

"Stop it!" yelled Eddie, who could take no more of Mortimer. "You evil man."

"Just imagine how much more evil I shall become once I have your imagination." Mortimer turned toward Beni. "And you—you call yourself a wizard? You can't even perform the simplest trick without your wand."

The wand! Suddenly everything seemed clear to Eddie. Thinking fast, he yelled, "The wand is on the table next to the big crystal ball."

Both Beni and Sandy ran for it. Mortimer, closest to Beni, tripped her and sent her sliding under the table upon which Eddie lay. Sandy ran around the table and reached the crystal ball. Standing on his tip-toes, he grabbed the wand.

Mortimer headed toward him, but the Sandman continued around the black slab. Running with wand in hand, Sandy slipped under Eddie's table. Mortimer retraced his steps to the other side. Eddie also turned that way to watch Sandy come out. But Sandy did not immediately appear. When he did, he held the wand in his opposite hand and came out at a different angle. He made straight for Mortimer's *Book of Spells* and began thumbing through it, repeating "Dispel Spells" to himself as he did so.

Mortimer moved toward Sandy and said, "Give me the wand, you foolish man. It can do you no good."

Mortimer walked past the black slab toward Sandy and away from Eddie. "Give it to me, I say."

"Ah, here it is," said Sandy. "The Ultimate Dispel Spell." He held the wand up high.

Then Sandy began to read:

Spells so evil, for evil cast
Shall now dispel and cease to last.
These spells, once strong, will all rebel
And loose the hold once held so well.
Reshape! Remake! And in good time.

"*To dispel my spells you need a rhyme,*" chanted Mortimer glibly.

"And you have given me that," said Sandy.

"Yes, little man, I have given you that," said Mortimer, "but you are no threat to me.

Besides, you have chosen the most difficult of all Dispel Spells: It attempts to dispel every spell I've ever cast. Now had you been a wizard, instead of a Sandman, I would never have given you a rhyme. As it is, yours was a noble, but useless, attempt."

Just then, while Eddie was watching Sandy, someone jumped up on his table. Turning to see who it was, Eddie was shocked to see Sandy.

"Sandy!"

Mortimer also turned, and turned back, and back again.

Sandy was standing on the table next to Eddie and Sandy was standing, wand in hand, next to the *Book of Spells*. Eddie was confused; it seemed impossible. Then he remembered he had seen this impossible scene before. Mortimer gathered it all in quickly and gasped in horror.

"The Deception!" Mortimer cringed.

As he said this, the Sandy who held the wand turned into Beni.

"Two can play the same game," she said.

"But how?" asked Mortimer.

"Simple," said Sandy. "I grabbed the wand, ran under the table and gave it to the lass."

"Then I pulled the Deception and ran out as Sandy," said Beni. "It was the only way I could think of to get the rhyme."

"The rhyme!" said a shocked Mortimer. "But surely you could not properly cast so powerful a spell."

"That's why I needed your power thrown in with mine," said Beni.

"Your spell cannot be strong enough," said Mortimer as if trying to convince himself. He flicked his wrists toward the crystals; nothing happened. He stared at his hands in disbelief. "No! It can't be."

He ran to look at his crystals, manually changing them to different scenes of Dreamland. Eddie looked, too. Poisoned River began to run beyond the waterfall at Beni's cave and flow into the Deserted Desert. Soon the river reached the edge of the Canyon of Death and began pouring into it.

"It can't be!" cried Mortimer, switching knobs again.

Eddie watched the flying sharks of Dire Straits—something was beginning to happen to them. Their wings shriveled and vanished, and they plunged into the sea. Mortimer dropped his head into his hands and issued a curse. "All of my hard work for nothing." All of his spells were being dispelled! (If Mortimer could cry, he surely would have now; but, since tears would kill him, he shed none.)

"We did it, we did it!" yelled an exuberant Sandman. He hugged Beni.

"Thank you, Beni," said Eddie. "Thank you all. You have helped me so much. I'll always remember you."

"Lad, you make it sound like a permanent farewell. And it shan't be that. That is, if you're ever willing to return to Dreamland—asleep, next time. Then I should be ever so happy to give you a proper tour."

"Oh, Sandy, I'd like to see you all again," said Eddie, "but I don't want to come back. Right now I just want to go home."

Turning to Marques, who still lay on the floor, Eddie said, "Marques, I think you've helped most of all. None of us would have made it this far without you."

"Thank you, Eddie," said the Giant, trying to push himself up. "You are my first true friend, and it was a pleasure and an honor to help you."

Then the most amazing transformation of all occurred—and right in that very room. Before Eddie's eyes, Marques began to grow in every direction until he was fully twice his size. "Wow!" said Eddie. At double his size, Marques looked very imposing indeed.

Mighty Marques let out a loud grunt as he tried and failed to push himself up.

"Can't you get up yet?" asked Eddie.

"No, I'm afraid I still can't."

Mortimer pointed over at Beni, yelling. "You wretched wizard, you shall pay for this! When my power returns, you shall pay!"

"But you shall be powerless until the last of your spells are dispelled," said Beni, "and I won't wait around that long."

"Yes, not until the last of my spells—" Suddenly Mortimer looked at the Giant. "He cannot get up yet! Of course!" said the warlock with renewed excitement. "The spells are being dispelled, but they are being dispelled chronologically! There is still time!" He rushed over to the table and grabbed the plunger-cap. He fastened it to his head and sneered: "I shall have his imagination yet! And the Imagination Transformation once completed, cannot be undone."

Eddie realized that he wasn't safe after all. Fear filled him anew.

"Mortimer," said Sandy, "even as we speak, the Canyon of Death is fillin' with water. Dark Castle rests on what was once— and what soon shall be—an underwater ledge. This whole place will be immersed in water. And water will be the death of you."

"And water isn't your biggest worry," added Marques. "When my strength returns, you won't want to be anywhere near me. Giants, you know, do not make idle threats."

"Once I have his imagination, I will conceive a way out of all of this," said Mortimer.

Suddenly the room filled with a blinking blue light and an electronic voice droning, "Blue Alert!"

"Get me home!" yelled Eddie.

"Hurry, Sandy, sprinkle your sleeping sand on him," said Beni.

"No, wait!" Marques said firmly. "We must make sure the tainted sand spell has been dispelled."

"How can we know?" asked Sandy.

Marques tapped his cheek. "I think I know. Get ready to do what Beni says, Sandy, but wait until I tell you to use the sand."

Sandy, still standing on the slab next to Eddie, grabbed a handful of sand. Mortimer, with cap on head, manually returned the crystals to Eddie's home. He grabbed the lever.

Eddie looked at the clocks, both still moved together. The Clock Lock hadn't yet been dispelled. Glancing back at the crystal, Eddie watched his mother walk into his room to wake him.

"Eddie, darling," his mother said as she neared her seemingly somnolent son. "Time to get up."

She lowered her hand to touch him.

"Now?" asked Sandy.

"Not yet," said Marques. "But ready yourself."

Mortimer began to pull the lever, shouting *"His imagination shall now be mine!"*

"No!" cried Eddie. As his mother's hand neared his shoulder, it slowed to one-seventh its speed.

"Now," yelled Marques. "Do it now, Sandy!"

"Close yer eyes, lad, so I can do this right," said Eddie's Sandman.

The last thing he saw before closing his eyes was Mortimer pulling the lever down. "No! No!" screamed Eddie.

19

EDDIE'S
FATE

Eddie felt the sand tickle his eyes, and he felt a sudden jolt. He opened his eyes, expecting to see the evil face of Mortimer; instead, he was looking at the loving face of his mother. The jolt he felt was simply her shaking his shoulder to wake him.

"It worked!" screamed Eddie.

"It's all right, darling," she said taking Eddie into her arms. "You were just having a bad dream."

"Oh, Mommy," said Eddie, "I love you. I'm so glad to see you."

"What's the matter?" said Eddie's father, who had heard his son screaming.

"Nothing," his mom said. "Eddie just had a nightmare, that's all."

"Oh, no, it wasn't a nightmare," said Eddie. "I was in Dreamland and I wasn't sleeping, though I looked like I was. Mortimer, the wicked witch of Dreamland, brought me there wide awake so that he could steal my imagination."

"Well, I'd say he'd have gotten a good one," his father joked.

"Three people saved my life," said Eddie.

"Saved your life?" asked his mom.

"Yeah. If Mortimer had stolen my imagination, I would have been dead. But Mortimer couldn't steal it until someone in the Real World tried to wake me up. That's why I was screaming."

"I see," said his mother without really seeing.

"Sandy, the Sandman who took me to Dreamland—"

"Sandy the Sandman, how cute," said his mom.

"I thought you said Mortimer brought you to Dreamland."

"No, Dad," said Eddie. "Mortimer cast a spell on Sandy's sand so that when Sandy took me to Dreamland I would be awake."

"Oh," said his dad.

Eddie hurried along barely stopping for breath: "Yeah, and . . . and we ran into Marques, the mightiest of all Giants. You

234

would have been amazed at him, Dad; he could knock Water Bugs clear out of sight with his club."

"Knock what clear out of sight?"

"Water Bugs. They were bugs that lived in the Poisoned River and curled themselves up like baseballs."

"Oh, like baseballs," said Eddie's mom, throwing a knowing look toward his father.

"Yeah, and we had to . . . well, you're not going to believe this part," Eddie cushioned his statement.

"Try us," his mom urged.

"Well, we had to find Beni the wizard to help us—"

"A wizard! Really now," said his mom.

"Oh, I knew you wouldn't believe it. But really there was a wizard. Only not at all the kind of wizard I would have imagined. No, this wizard was just a little girl. Kind of pretty, though. And she was a good wizard. She saved my life."

Eddie's mom turned to his dad and said, "See what happens when he stays up late? He has bad dreams and imagines that they are real."

"You don't believe me, do you?" asked Eddie.

"Oh, honey," his mother said, "it's not a question of whether I believe you. I love you lots. But sometimes the mind plays tricks on us; especially when we're young, and we imagine all kinds of wild and wonderful things. I give you credit, your story is imaginative. It makes me proud that you created it all yourself, knowingly or unknowingly."

"But it's true, every word," said Eddie.

"Honey, think about it. How could you have been there when you were here in your bed?"

"I know, Mom, it's a paradox—"

"A what?" said his mom.

"A paradox. It's when something seems—"

"Your mother and I know what a paradox is."

"Oh," said Eddie.

"We were just surprised that you knew such a big word," said his mom.

"Well, I didn't until Sandy explained it to me."

"Sandy the Sandman," said his mom.

"Yeah," confirmed Eddie. "He explained how it looked like I was asleep when I was really wide awake in Dreamland. I know it's hard to understand."

"Well, we're trying hard to understand," said his dad with a smile.

236

"Wait a minute!" said Eddie, jumping out of bed. "I can *prove* it!"

"How can you prove it?" asked Eddie's father.

"Remember the baseball cards we got last night?"

"Sure."

"Well, I gave Joe Ortiz's card to Marques."

"You gave away your favorite card?" his father asked.

"Yeah, see, Marques was sad 'cause he was a small Giant. At least, he thought he was small. You should have seen him, Dad; he must have been ten feet tall—twenty when Mortimer's spell was broken. Anyway, I gave him Joe Ortiz's card 'cause he thought it was funny that a Giant was only five-nine. Here, let me show you my cards."

Eddie pulled out his cards and went through them one by one. "See! Joe Ortiz's card isn't here!"

"Oh, honey, it probably fell out of your pocket," said his mom.

Eddie's expression changed from jubilation to frustration.

"But it happened, really it did."

"I think we've heard enough, young man," said his mother.

Eddie thought his proof convincing; yet his parents still did not believe him. Maybe if he'd told them the truth about the science project, maybe then they'd believe him. Maybe none of this would have happened at all if he had been truthful about that in the first place. He resolved to tell them about it now.

"I bet you're hungry after all of your adventures. How 'bout I fix you some bacon and eggs real quick?" his mother said, glancing at her watch.

When she looked at her watch, Eddie remembered about going to Grandma's. If he told his parents about the project now, he wouldn't get to go; he'd be forced to work on it. And he'd be able to finish it all on Sunday. He was sure he would. It would be good to tell his parents everything, but it could wait until tomorrow.

"After I eat, I'll get ready to go to Grandma's."

"Good," said his mom. "Wait. How did you know we were going to Grandma's? I was planning to surprise you. John, did you tell him?"

Eddie's father shook his head, "I wouldn't dare ruin one of your surprises, sweetheart. I certainly know better than that."

"Then how did you know, Eddie?" his mom asked.

"It doesn't matter . . . ," Eddie began, and as he did he almost heard Princess Josefina's voice floating back to him: *It does not matter what your parents will or will not believe. What matters is that you return and have the chance to tell them. What matters is that you believe.* He realized that the princess was right; even as he finished speaking, he knew it. "It doesn't matter. You wouldn't believe it, anyway."

His dad smiled: "Somehow I believe that."

His mother smiled, too. So did Eddie.

"I'm so happy to be home," said Eddie, hugging first his mom and then his dad.

THE END

ABOUT THE AUTHOR

John Duel was born on June 16, 1960. A graduate from Santa Clara University, he currently resides in southern California. *Wide Awake in Dreamland* is his first novel.